WHEN THINGS COME TO LIGHT

Some things never come to light: many have been delivered:
but more hath been swallowed up in obscurity
and the caverns of oblivion
– Thomas Browne (1605–82)

For Luke, Ronan, Sam and Emily

INTRODUCTION

In every family there is someone who records the past, for whom the continuity of history matters. Long before the study of genealogy became fashionable, my mother's sister, Margaret, was fascinated by her family history. On marriage, she moved to England and rarely came back to Northern Ireland, and yet, when she died, she left boxes of papers, random letters, official documents and recorded family memories she had collected over decades.

My mother didn't talk about her past. Poring over the faded letters and old photographs my aunt had collected, I learnt, for the first time, about my mother's family. Her father's people came from north Antrim: McKays and Pinkertons who lived in the townland of Seacon near the town of Ballymoney. They adhered to the principles of Unitarianism: independence of thought, universal brotherhood. Liberty, Equality, Fraternity. They were Dissenters who stood outside the mainstream of public opinion and followed the French *philosophes*. Once their small community had flourished. Over time, the pull of city life, emigration, a low marriage rate and a hardening of political positions after the partition of Ireland in 1921 depleted their congregation. My great-aunt Bessie, who lived much of her life in Ballymoney, was once asked why she never married. When her turn came, she answered cheerfully: there were no male cousins left. Another old bachelor, when posed the same question, said that, when the time came for him to marry, there were no first cousins left and no second cousins either. 'And you'd hardly expect me', he said, 'to go with a stranger.'

Eventually the Unitarian church in Ballymoney was closed. The building was demolished to make way for the local district council offices. The last name on the birth register of the church is that of John Pinkerton. John is now a man in late middle age, retired from a successful legal practice. I met him for the first time when researching this book. Our family connection is tenuous: he and I share a great-great-grandmother: a woman called Nancy Pinkerton. In the sleepy townlands surrounding the town of Ballymoney I didn't meet anyone else related to me.

As a child I never knew my maternal grandparents. In the year they died, I was twenty years old. At that age I didn't care: I had other priorities. It is only now, when I have grandchildren of my own, that I am conscious that Wallace and Margaret McKay form a link with my past. A link that was broken years before I was born. The source of the rupture between my mother and her parents belongs to a different era in Ireland, but the years that followed haven't lessened its impact. In 1908, for the first time, canon law required that for a marriage between a Catholic and a non-Catholic to be valid the children must be raised in the Catholic faith. Over the sixty-two years of its imposition, the *Ne Temere* decree did untold damage to Protestant/Catholic relations.

It split families. Mine included.

In writing this book, I wanted to learn about my history; to understand the family influences that make me who I am and, in particular, to retrieve my grandparents from 'the canyons of oblivion.' When I started out, I realised that sticking to the known facts – as writers are often advised to do – would take the story only so far. The information gleaned from my aunt's papers is a foundation: that is all. In transforming fact into fiction, I had to depend on my imagination to build the rising walls and floors; the windows, doors and roof.

I

Dublin 1905

Four ducks waddle up from the pond to where the young couple sit on a bench in St Stephen's Green. The woman is dressed in a navy skirted costume, fitted at the waist, and she is wearing a wide-brimmed hat. She has a long face and a generous mouth. The sharp blue of her eyes is a magnet. She picks a handful of breadcrumbs from the paper bag on her lap. Her lace-gloved hand arches above her head as the crumbs spray out. She is aware of the grace of her movements and its effect on the man sitting beside her. The ducks compete with gulls swooping down to snatch the breadcrumbs.

'Look, Wallace, how they fight!'

He stretches his arm along the bench back. 'That is Nature's way.'

'Oh, but it is so cruel.'

'Nature is neither cruel nor kind. It simply is what is. Charles Darwin has shone his light on the way the world works.'

Her expression is inscrutable. 'Adam and Eve have no part in our creation?'

'My dear, are you disappointed when I tell you the story of Eden is a legend, not to be taken literally?'

'Not if you tell me so.'

Is she teasing him? He can never be sure with Margaret.

'Do you know what St Paul said?'

She shakes her head.

'You should do, Maggie.'

'If you call me Maggie. I'll start calling you Wally.'

He smiles. 'You may call me anything you wish.'

She sprinkles breadcrumbs into his cupped palm as he continues.

'St Paul says, *"I will not permit a woman to teach or have dominion over man but to be in quietness, for Adam was first formed and then Eve, and Adam was not beguiled, the woman being beguiled hath fallen into transgression."'*

A vague, manly heat wafts out of the tweed folds of his coat and brings a blush to her cheeks. *If only he knew ...* To be beguiled is her unspoken desire.

As Wallace rubs his hands, a few crumbs fall to the ground. A sparrow skitters in under his feet. His voice is soft so as not to disturb the bird. 'Too many crimes have been committed against women in the name of Eve and one talkative serpent.'

Often when she is with Wallace, Margaret feels that he is the teacher while she is the student. He knows so much about the world and she is free to ask him any question she likes. Except the one question that she can never ask. His mind she can fathom, but what of his heart? Wallace is invariably courteous, yet abstracted, as if his thoughts are concentrated elsewhere. On her next birthday she'll be twenty-nine-years-old. Not old compared to some but old all the same. Her mother has said to her more than once, 'you need to pull up that line before the fish gets away.'

Margaret has trained herself to overcome her natural will to *have dominion* – as St Paul would have it. Her years of teaching in the schoolroom have led her to expect acquiescence from the children in her care, but such an attitude will not endear her to Wallace. Brittle with anticipation, she brushes her hand against his. A cold wind picks up and Wallace suggests that they retire to take tea. She crumples up the empty paper bag and slips it into her purse. Seeing her pinched white face, he wonders if she is feeling alright. It's the chilly air, nothing more, she says, wondering if she is wasting her time. It takes all her strength not to cry out in exasperation as they stroll towards the park gates.

In the Oriental café they dawdle over tea and scones. Beyond the steamed-up window, the street outside is a blur. The pot of tea has gone cold. At the sound of his voice, she turns back to look at him. Her mother's advice: always give a man your full attention.

'And on Saturdays there is a concert and food stall. It's so jolly.'

Sea baths hold a fascination for Wallace. This isn't the first time he has begged her to visit the Merrion Pier Baths with him, although she has never agreed to go. She waits for him to ask, conscious that her knees are almost touching his long legs stretched out under the tablecloth.

'Margaret, dear, will you come with me?'

'It sounds a little unhealthy.'

'Nonsense. It's very clean. There's a pump run on gas that is operated each day to replace the sea water. An establishment of the highest quality.'

'I'm sure it is.'

'Your modesty will be protected, I assure you. You know that I wouldn't invite you, otherwise.'

She sighs. It is true: he is a perfect gentleman.

'Of my own dignity, I can't be so sure. I'm afraid I can't swim a stroke. Never learnt how, you see.'

'Why, Wallace, I am surprised to hear that.'

The smile dancing around her mouth makes him want to kiss her, but he fears she might be offended. He lifts her hand. So lightly, his mouth is a moth landing on her fingers.

'And I thought,' she murmurs, 'that you knew everything.'

He is so eager that she cannot refuse him outright.

'Oh Wallace, I don't know. Let me think about it.'

And he has to be satisfied that she has not said no.

II

He has known from the beginning: his first sight of her walking up the centre aisle of the Unitarian church on St Stephen's Green. Dressed in sober grey, a line of school-children following her. Since he started at the College of Science in Dublin, Wallace attends the church on Sundays. It is his link with his homeplace in Seacon. That day, when he pushes open the church door, an old man seated in a pew raises his hand in salute.

'Seymour is my name. You're welcome, young man.' The old man says, his fingers trembling on a silver-topped cane, and beside him, is Mrs Seymour, her little face peeking from under a mildew-speckled hat. The old man reminds Wallace of his father: his leathery neck and enormous hands, his slow unblinking stare. Despite his frailty, Mr Seymour displays the same spirit of endurance. Wallace stops to talk to them and the old woman rests her gloved hand on his sleeve. She asks if he would sit with them but, at that moment, he is distracted by the sight of a young woman walking up the centre aisle of the church, at the head of a line of children. She ushers the children into their pews.

When she turns around, she startles Wallace with the bounty of her smile.

From the pulpit, the minister exhorts the congregation: 'Let us rejoice in the great liberty that is ours. All science, all research are friends and allies of the Truth.'

Wallace quells a desire to cheer. Without a doubt, the minister is a man of intelligence and oratory. By comparison, the Unitarian minister at home, in County Antrim, is a dullard. After the service is over, cups of tea and biscuits are served in the schoolroom downstairs.

'Let me introduce to you to Miss Margaret Minnis,' Mr Seymour says, as he ushers Wallace towards the young teacher. When Wallace bends to shake her hand, her fearless gaze makes him wonder if she knows the effect she is having on him.

'Your father waited too long to marry.'

Through the window Wallace sees the byre crumbling into ruin, stone on stone, and the bent, lichened apple trees in the orchard: a familiar scene from his childhood. The old farmhouse in Seacon where he was born and where he doesn't belong anymore. He turns back to his mother. 'Margaret's father has a farm outside Ballygowan.'

'Do I know it?'

'In County Down, and you'll be glad to know they are Non-Subscribing folk like ourselves.'

'It's time you settled down. I want to see my grandchildren before I die.'

Wallace smiles.

The house is full of dust and worn-out belongings. The place is falling apart. Whenever he sees a newspaper advertisement for a new washtub or a newly-invented household device he thinks of his mother: how worn and wasted she has become. One day he will be in a position to repair the farmhouse. Maybe to replace it altogether with a new house, solidly built and with modern conveniences.

'What would you think of that, Mam?'

Vaguely she looks around the room. 'The old house can fall around my ears, Wallace. I only want to see my grandchildren.'

'How is Anna doing with her studies?' he asks, to distract her. Anna, his sister, next to him in age, has finally got her way and is in Belfast studying to be a teacher. No thanks to him. He should try harder to look after his brothers and sisters. He is the eldest, after all.

'Anna is doing better than we expected. She has a will of iron and not a whit of sense.'

He thinks of two cousins, Sam and himself, lying on a river bank, watching for fish in the water. Their last day together in Seacon before one of them left for Honolulu. Will he and Sam ever meet again?

'Sam Pinkerton used to say he had two kinds of sense: common sense and nonsense.'

She chuckles. 'Aye, so he does too. The letters he sends his mother. He can't spell for toffee. That reminds me,' she opens the drawer of the dresser and takes out an envelope. 'Anna wrote to me yesterday, says she has been offered a position in England when she finishes her studies. I'd rather she came home but all the same ...'

Relief in her voice: one daughter on her way and the others coming behind. With the way things are and so few young men about, she says, maybe no grandchildren from that quarter either. Which brings the conversation around to him again and when might she meet his bride-to-be?

'I'll bring Margaret to Seacon to meet you, but only if she says yes.'

She stares. 'And why wouldn't she?'

In the end, the weather turns bad and he invites Margaret to accompany him to the Botanic Gardens instead of the sea baths.

'Oh, how beautiful it is!' she says, her face pressed against the window of the tram. The partially-covered monument in the street reminds her of the drawing of the Pharos of Alexandria in a textbook. A sand-coloured towering presence: one of the wonders of the Ancient World. As the tram swings past, the legend carved into the stone is clear enough for Wallace to read aloud: *'No man has a right to fix the boundary to the march of a nation.'*

Her expression hardens. 'He got his comeuppance.'

Wallace murmurs, 'Poor Mr Parnell.'

'Poor Mr Parnell brought disgrace to a noble cause.'

'Can't you find it in your heart?'

'Never!' Narrowing her lips and gripping her purse. 'And she a married woman, with responsibilities.'

'My dear, I think the cause of Ireland will triumph whether you forgive Mr Parnell or not.'

Slyly he waits for her reaction: he loves to see her passion flaming. She does not disappoint him. As if in prayer, she clasps her hands. 'To see Ireland free and independent is all that matters. I only hope the will of the people is not broken.'

'I hope so too.'

Wallace has matters other than nationhood on his mind. They travel through the streets of Dublin until they come to their destination and alight at the gates of the Botanic Gardens. There are flowers edging the lawns and shrubbery. In the distance, a curvilinear glasshouse is framed by trees. Between the flowerbeds, a gravel path leads into woodland.

'Oh Wallace!' She spins around. 'I had no idea that such a place existed.'

'Come along,' he chivvies her along the path, past the herbaceous borders and down the steps between the pines. 'Now close your eyes.'

Giggling, she obeys.

'Take my arm and let me lead you.'

She stumbles from time to time, leaning in close enough to feel the touch of his coat on her cheek.

'Now, Margaret, you can take a look.'

For a moment, the whiteness dazzles her. A tree spreads its branches of dark green leaves and cascading flowers. Petals, folded like squares of linen, tremble in the breeze. They remind her of a clothesline of washing, but the tree is prettier than laundry. Each flower is delicate; each whispering movement of leaf and petal is pure delight.

'Oh, Wallace!'

He holds her hand. Without speaking, they gaze at the tree. This is the moment, he thinks. This is the perfect time.

'*Davidia Involucrata*,' he says instead. 'The only member of its genus. It is a native of China and was brought halfway across the world to Kew Gardens. An unfortunate young Englishman almost died in his quest to find a specimen. And now the tree has taken root in Dublin. Look at it, Margaret, and tell me what the flowers remind you of.'

She rests her chin on her hand. A pigeon coos somewhere in the woods.

'Pocket handkerchiefs?'

'Precisely!' He blushes with excitement. 'It's even known as the pocket handkerchief tree.' He reaches up to touch the luminous surfaces of the flowers. 'Sometimes it's called the dove tree or the ghost tree.'

He is like a child, she thinks, acting as if he brought the tree across the world all by himself.

'Have you ever seen anything so exquisite?'

Just then, a drop of rain falls on her cheek. 'Oh dear, we're in for a wetting.'

She is glad to have a reason to distract him. He takes her arm and together they scramble back along the steps as the rain starts to beat down. When they reach the path, they can see the tea rooms far away across the lawns.

'We'll be drenched!' she wails.

'Let's shelter in here,' he says, lifting a branch of a giant pine tree. He leads her by the hand into the clearing around the gnarled tree trunk. A secret place, where the air smells woody and old and the ground is thick with pine needles. Above their heads is a canopy of matted branches. He is reminded of Seacon.

'How dry it is.' She unpins her hat and shakes the droplets off it. Her words sound small, inconsequential. Standing close to him, she is conscious of a new intimacy; as if everyone else has been scattered by the deluge and they are the only people left. Adam and Eve in the Garden, she thinks, with a slight shiver. His face is white in the gloom, the look in his eyes so intense, she asks without thinking, 'What is the matter?'

'Margaret,' he is hesitant, his hand clasping hers. Should he kneel?

She waits.

'Will you honour me by becoming my wife?'

Surely, he isn't serious! Not here under a dripping tree and her hair in such a state. To want something for so long and then to have it land in her lap. Be sensible, she tells herself. What did she expect? Choirs of angels, blaring trumpets, thunder and lightning? Wallace has chosen a day in mourning to make his declaration: a day of black clouds swollen with rain. How typical of a man, she thinks, how annoying. Then, almost immediately, a feeling of exultation. Mrs Wallace McKay, at last. She must write to her mother this evening. How pleased she will be! *You should keep that one,* her mother has said of Wallace, *he looks like a horse.*

'Oh, yes, I will,' she says and then stupidly. 'Thank you.'

Wallace is dizzy with relief. He takes her in his arms. The damp air moistening the greenery, deepens the shades of leaf and mould wrapping around them as they kiss. The prospect of a new life unrolls before her: husband, children, a house of her own. She trembles with excitement, and, yet, the touch of his lips on hers cannot dispel her vague sense of disappointment. It lingers long after the rain stops, and Wallace and Margaret pass through the gates of the Botanic Gardens to walk out into the world together.

After they are married and have moved into the new house in St Kevin's Park in Dublin, Margaret gives Wallace a tin box. Inside, he finds her birth certificate, a copy of her father's will, her teacher's diploma, a variety of documents. At the bottom of the box is a notebook. The first few pages are covered in her father's spidery handwriting: details of births and deaths and scraps of family history. He is about to put it away when the last entry catches his attention. *It is thought that the informer James Minnis, who turned King's evidence after the Rebellion of '98, was a distant relation of ours.*

The following pages are blank.

From then on, Wallace takes delight in teasing Margaret. 'While my kin were out fighting for Liberty, one of yours betrayed them to the gibbet.'

She won't be drawn. 'That's all in the past. The sooner Ireland's independence is won, the better.'

'I wonder ...'

She interrupts him. 'You know I wonder too, sometimes, if you're as true to the cause as your forebears were.'

Wallace refuses to take umbrage. 'I will never shed blood, if that is what you mean.'

They are sitting in the drawing room. The curtains are drawn and, in the firelight, shadows dance in the room. She puts down the piece of embroidery on which she is working. 'No, I don't want that, either.'

'Well, then?'

'It seems to me,' she says, 'that you have a weakness for things English. It makes me despair of you.'

For a moment he is silenced by her effrontery. Then, with a fervour that startles them both, he says, 'The English genius is incomparable.'

'I am only saying.'

Anger builds inside him. 'No nation on earth has given the world so much.'

'Heavens above!' she cries, 'are we to be grateful for the British Empire, the Great Hunger, for Earl Cornwallis?'

'Of course not, but no imperialist excess can take from the fact that Francis Bacon was English and Isaac Newton, and Robert Boyle, and Charles Darwin. They are great men of science.'

Such an outburst goes against his nature, his sense of decorum. In conversation he prefers to use reason over religion, persuasion over passion in order to make a point. He takes out his handkerchief, dabs his mouth and waits. In her condition she should not be agitated. Dear Margaret! And to think her confinement is only weeks away.

'My dearest, I apologise for raising my voice.'

Margaret picks up the embroidery hoop, knots a thread and bites it off with her teeth. She rummages in her sewing box for another skein of embroidery thread.

'At the very least, Wallace,' she says, 'you might have the grace to acknowledge that Mr Boyle was an Irishman.'

He breathes a sigh of relief. Living with Margaret has taught him that there is a price to pay for her spirited, at times, exhilarating company. She has, he has learnt, a ferocious temper. On rare occasions he has been at the receiving end, but she tends to reserve her bile for the servants or the tradesmen. Already, since they have moved into St Kevin's Park, one maid has given in her notice.

Six months later, when Margaret comes down from the nursery after settling Maggie, their new baby, Wallace shows her the letter from his mother:

> I dreamt one night before your last letter that one of the Mr Minnis's brought your baby and dumped her into my lap and said, There keep you that, and went off, lighthearted. I was so superstitious that I was for writing to Margaret on the next day to see how you were all getting on.

'After all her talk of grandchildren! I'm tempted to write and ask why she is so afraid of our little baby being dumped on her.'

Margaret is not amused. To her, the letter holds a secret message that, as far as her mother-in-law is concerned, nobody is good enough for Eliza McKay's oldest son. In particular, not Margaret, née Minnis. She takes up her knitting and Wallace goes back to reading the newspaper, but he can't concentrate. Out of his pocket he fishes a letter from Sam Pinkerton in Hawaii: *John, you mite just as well see some of the world when young, as not for when you grow old.* Why, Wallace wonders, is this ferocious dissatisfaction gnawing in my gut?

'The cat, dearest.'

He looks down. The animal has wrapped around itself at his feet and is gazing up at him, miaowing. He scoops up the animal and carries it down the corridor to the kitchen where it hops out of his arms and starts to scratch at the back door. 'Calm down. I'll let you out.'

As the cat disappears into the darkness, Wallace thinks of the things he wants to do: to explore the world, to build a house for his parents, to have a son who will carry on his name. More than anything, he wants to be free. Anna would understand. His sister has the determination to be more than what is expected of her. She is living in Shropshire but, from her letters, Wallace knows that it's only a matter of time before she moves on. To Canada, she writes, or maybe South Africa. He yearns to confide in her but, instead, finds himself writing to her about Margaret and the baby, the recent visit of his younger sister and their mother, and how well their brother James is doing, training to be a doctor. Nothing that his sister would not know already.

III

They are out for an evening together, just the two of them, a rare enough occurrence these days. When the tram arrives, it is full of passengers but a gentleman stands up, tipping his hat and offers Margaret his seat. Wallace stands next to her until, at the next stop, two workmen alight from the tram. As the two of them sit, side by side in the vacated seats, an awkwardness descends as if they are strangers thrown together.

'Are you warm enough, my dear?'

Her hand, in its lavender glove, rests on her purse. Her face is as placid as a meadow in summer.

'I do hope that the baby won't fret,' she says, unable to extricate herself fully from home, the skewed gaze of little Maggie and the new baby Elizabeth's colic.

'I have a surprise for you,' he says.

Her eyebrows arch and her mouth twitches into a smile.

'This evening the dinner will amaze you. It will be unlike any you have ever had before.'

'I can't imagine what you mean,' she says, 'but I promise you I will eat it. I'm hungry enough to eat a horse.'

He likes her plain speaking, her willingness to meet a challenge. Soon, he thinks, she will need every ounce of that courage.

In Sackville Street, she saunters beside him, her arm hooked into his, the skirt of her blue taffeta dress swinging under her coat. Two bony Ulster folk, as he describes Margaret and himself in his letter to Sam Pinkerton who has now left Hawaii for the mining fields of North Dakota. Wait until he hears my news, Wallace thinks, as he and Margaret walk through the bustling crowds, past shop windows and bellowing street boys carrying bundles of newspapers.

And, he thinks, when *she* hears his news.

Margaret tugs on his arm. 'Look!'

The glow of gas lights outside, brass and mahogany, a glimpse of cut-glass chandeliers inside. An agricultural adviser on his salary cannot afford the luxury of dining at the Gresham Hotel. She knows that. To his annoyance, he sees her mouth tighten.

'Just a little farther, my dear.'

Down the street, he stops in front of a heavily-carved entrance and pushes open the door to let her pass in front of him. Margaret steps into the dining room and finds herself in an Aladdin's cave, dazzled by a richness of colour and mirrored surfaces. Above her head, a canopy of bright silk billows out in streams of red and gold; wall lights in shades of blue and green cast a glow on ornate tapestries.

'Oh!' is all she can say.

The tables are set for dinner with white tablecloths; each has a centrepiece of flowers floating in a burnished copper bowl. A man dressed in silk trousers and an embroidered jacket of cloth of gold comes forward to meet them. His skin is toffee-brown and he is wearing a turquoise-coloured turban.

'You are welcome, dear lady and gentleman,' the palms of his hands coming together in greeting. 'My name is Karim Khan.'

As if in a dream, she sits down. Another couple is already seated at an adjacent table. Otherwise, the dining room is empty, apart from a waiter standing behind a pillar. Clicking his fingers for the waiter to come forward to take their coats, Karim Khan tells them, 'Tonight you will dine on dishes fit for a Moghul prince.'

'Steady on, old boy.' Wallace laughs up at him. He has been here before, Margaret realises with surprise. The Indian continues to speak in his sing-song intonation, and the man's velvety voice edges inside Margaret's clothes. She tightens her knees, clutches the purse on her lap.

'The Moghuls of long ago brought their food to a great height. Roghan josh, mutanjan pulao, qeema matar. Try them, dear lady and gentleman, and you will agree that they are princely dishes.'

'He's right, you know,' Wallace says. 'You'll never eat one of those insipid liquids that we call curry again.'

'Kari is for bad meat. In northern India we only use good meat, best chickens. Please, dear lady, have a *papad*.'

Gingerly she takes the crisp, flat bread and breaks off a piece.

'It won't poison you, Margaret.'

It has, she discovers, a pleasant, delicate texture. She takes another piece and munches it.

'Don't eat too much of that,' Wallace cautions. 'You have a banquet ahead of you.'

A banquet she could never have imagined: steaming bowls of chunks of meat in fiery red sauces, vegetables in light batter, chickpeas, garlic, rice, ginger, garam masala, cardamon, saffron: spices she has never heard of. Tastes roll around in her mouth and are vanquished by a new wave of flavours.

The two of them are like children, captivated by the foreignness of the place, the exotic tastes. She samples every dish, even the one made with hot chilli that causes her to moan. His admiration of her is so fervid that she feels her skin humming with excitement. The sight of her blushes, in turn, arouses him and he wants to take her in his arms there and then. To plunge together into the darkness beyond their glittering lair.

He leans towards her. 'I have something to tell you.'

His tone so solemn, she is on her guard immediately.

'What is it?'

Wallace spreads his hands out on the white damask tablecloth. 'You remember I spoke to you about my relation Lieutenant Megaw?'

She stares at him, puzzled.

'I am glad to say that he has spoken up for me and, as a consequence, I have been offered a position, a very good one actually, with a house and servants. And we will have more than enough to live on. You will be a lady of leisure, my darling.'

In his voice, she senses danger. She waits as he talks, about how Lieutenant Megaw, his good friend and mentor, recommended him – despite his lack of experience – to be a visiting agent for the Assam Company.

'He even told them I excelled in my studies and was a fine catch and, if they did not employ me, there were others who would gladly do so.' He takes a sip of water. 'The old house at Seacon is in an awful state and, now that I can afford it, I intend to have a new house built. The Lord knows the old folk deserve some comfort.'

She has never seen him so alive, so charged with excitement. The name of the Assam Company means nothing to her.

She is filled with foreboding. 'Forgive me, Wallace, but I don't understand.'

He is concentrating on his news, on the great leap of his heart as he articulates aloud the secret he has carried inside him for weeks. Margaret will be glad, he knows, once she understands what this means for him and for his future. He provides for Margaret and the children, as is his duty but, all the while, he is suffocating. He will show Sam Pinkerton that he is not afraid to venture into the unknown and, what is more, to bring his wife and children with him. What a jolly time they will have.

'What are you saying? Are we leaving Dublin?'

'We will be leaving for Calcutta in two months.'

'Calcutta!'

She rears up from the table, her arms outstretched, her breasts heaving under the blue taffeta, her mouth distorted, her eyes sparking with rage, shrieking, '*Have you lost your senses?*'

A plate crashes onto the floor.

Not for the first time, her extreme nature shocks him. On their wedding day, her brother, the worse for wear, insisted on taking him aside to say that Margaret had a temper bigger than herself. At the time Wallace ignored him, the alcohol on his breath, the trickle of saliva on his chin. Later he witnessed Margaret's outbursts: her rage directed at tradesmen, or Petty, the domestic servant, even, occasionally, the cat. But she has never lost her temper in public before. He is appalled at the unseemly display.

'Margaret, compose yourself this instant!'

She ignores him, her voice resonating around the dining room. It is fortunate, Wallace thinks, that the other couple have left and that they are alone. At the sound of disturbance, Karim Khan rushes out from the kitchen while the waiter and the cook peer around the curtain.

'Dear lady,' the Indian pleads, 'I beg you, say what we have done to offend you.'

Margaret raises her arm as if to strike him. Then she crumples, covering her mouth to stifle a scream. In sympathy, the Indian shakes his head and cries, 'Oh, oh, oh!'

Despite his mortification, Wallace feels a bubble of laughter rise up his throat.

'Mr Khan, please don't alarm yourself,' he says. 'My wife has been startled by some news. That is all.'

It takes a while before Mr Khan is reassured. Eventually he claps his hands and shoos the waiter and cook back into the kitchen. Then he withdraws, backwards, his body bent into an exaggerated bow as he disappears behind the kitchen curtain.

Wallace slumps in his chair and closes his eyes.

'Servants, you said.'

'What?'

'You said servants.'

Warily, he opens his eyes.

Margaret dabs her mouth with her napkin. She is business-like. 'Exactly how many servants do you think we will have?'

IV

'To say goodbye to my oldest child is hard enough, but to go to the other side of the world and take your two little babies with you, is too much to bear.'

Hysteria builds in his mother's voice.

'Mam, pull yourself together. Margaret is here and the girls. They mustn't see you like this.'

His wife is walking across the yard, the baby Elizabeth in her arms and little Maggie at her side. His mother straightens up. With the corner of her apron she wipes her eyes.

Her welcome is faint. 'Dear Margaret.'

'That's better,' he says heartily. It isn't like his mother to let her feelings get the better of her. She should be glad for his sake. For her own sake too, come to think of it: the new house will be built now. Thanks to his brother James's undertakings, the work will go ahead.

'In five years' time we will be home from India on leave. I'll look forward to seeing the new house. You must write often and tell me about its progress.'

It feels strange to sit in the parlour and take tea as if they are strangers, but his mother insists. She pours out tea in the good china and offers them seed cake from the cake stand. The quiet scene is disrupted when his sister Anna strides into the room.

He stands up. 'I see you came home.'

'I came home,' she flashes him a dark look. 'But nobody put out the good tea service for me.'

'Now, now,' his mother says.

Anna walks agitatedly around the room, addressing each one in turn. 'Good day brother Wallace, good day Margaret, and good day baby in the cradle, what a dotey, and good day to you, lovely Maggie.'

She enfolds the little girl in her embrace. Children love Anna, Wallace thinks. She is a bit of a child herself. You never knew quite where you were with her.

'Because of you,' she tells the little girl as she swings her around, 'I've been told that I'm no longer permitted to slide down the banisters. Giving a bad example apparently.'

Maggie shrieks with laughter as she whirls.

'Stop that, Anna,' Margaret says, 'you'll make her dizzy.'

Anna sits down beside her brother and pulls the child onto her lap.

'Anna, what happened to your position? I thought you liked it.'

'I refuse to say another word about it.' Her tone is theatrical. 'All I can say is I was treated abominably.'

'I think ...'

'I couldn't care less what you think, Wallace.' She covers her ears with her hands and jumps up, 'Come on, Maggie, let's go and feed the chickens.'

Without Anna, the conversation is desultory: about the weather, the trip that is facing them, how his father is over at McLean's helping out with the building of a barn and will return in a while. Later when Margaret settles in the parlour to feed the baby, he stands by the sink in the kitchen while his mother washes the dishes.

'Tell me, how is Anna really? She seems a little strange.'

His mother sighs. 'Ach, she has her good days. And her bad. Today because you're all here she's wayward. Tomorrow she might not leave her bed till noon. Her poor father is driven distracted. He's working from daybreak till night while she is a lie-abed. She suffers with her nerves, I tell him.'

'When she finds a new position she'll settle down.'

'Maybe. You know she has plans to travel to Canada.'

A change of scenery, he is certain, is exactly what Anna needs.

His mother drops her voice to a whisper. 'Do you know what she's doing now?'

He waits.

'I found her in her bedroom, writing.'

He is mystified. 'Is that bad?'

She shakes her head. 'She told me she was writing a poem.'

'It's not against the law, Mam.'

His mother lifts a plate out of the soapy water and puts it on the draining rack.

'Anna is a strange girl,' Wallace soothes, 'but there is no harm in her.'

No matter what he says, his mother is unconvinced. 'Writing poetry in this house! It is just not right.'

'Anna will settle down.'

Crying, his mother doesn't hear him, twisting the cloth fiercely in her hands. 'Wallace, tell me, where is it going to end?'

When the time comes for them to leave, his father, to his surprise, grasps him by the shoulders and pulls him close. He surrenders to the dark, familiar smells of him, the tang of manure and smoke. Eyes watering, he takes the baby out of Margaret's arms and holds her up for his parents to kiss. They all walk up to the gate at the top of the lane. Standing in a huddle, his mother, father and Anna see them off. They wave and wave until the hackney cab turns the corner and they can fall back into their seats.

'Well, I'm glad that is over,' Margaret says.

Wallace lifts her hand to his lips. 'Aye,' he says, 'I'm glad too.'

V

For the first week of the voyage Wallace is seasick. To his chagrin, neither his wife nor his daughters show any sign of being affected by the swell. He is corralled in the cabin with the baby in her cot while Margaret and little Maggie explore every part of the ship and carry back tales of life on board. His daughter wants to tell him about the pretty lady with a family of boys they had met in the dining room who are travelling as far as Port Said.

'We're going to see Egypt, Daddy,' she says, as she bounces on the edge of his bed and wakes up the baby. 'Mummy says so.'

'Margaret, have pity on me,' he implores.

The two of them go off again while he falls back into his pillows and waits for the baby to stop bawling.

By the time Wallace has found his sea legs the ship is about to dock in the port of Gibraltar. On deck he finds Margaret sitting on a slatted chair, the little girl beside her and the baby on her knee. She is holding an atlas with its pages open. Mother and child are following the track of her finger on the map.

'We're between two great seas now,' he tells them. 'Behind us is the Atlantic Ocean and ahead is the Mediterranean Sea.'

Margaret gazes at him from under her straw hat. 'You need fattening up, my dear. You've lost an awful weight.'

He sinks on the chair beside her. 'And they say women are the weaker sex.'

'Only men say that.'

He chuckles. There is a sensuousness about the moment: the high blue sky, the sleeve of her silk dress fluttering in the breeze and settling on the flesh of her arm. In all the time he has known her he has never seen her so content.

He takes her hand. 'Are you happy, my dear?'

She smiles. 'Look at the mountains. How red and fiery they are, not like the ones at home, and those white houses and dark trees. Oh, what I would give to paint a picture of it.'

'You're not sorry I took you away from Ireland?'

'I am not sorry, no.'

'What do you wish for?'

She looked thoughtful. 'That our daughters grow up to be gifted young women. And that they will live in an Ireland that is free.'

Holding the baby in the crook of his arm, Wallace walks to the rail to gaze at the port of Gibraltar. Margaret comes to stand beside him.

'And what do you wish for?'

'I want a son.'

But she is already distracted. 'Oh, I forgot to tell you that I met the most lovely people last night at dinner, Mr and Mrs Caldwell from Larne, would you believe! They promised to teach us bridge if we make up a four. Please, say we can go.'

Dreamlike, the days merge beyond the bounds of time. Little Maggie follows her mother's instructions and extends the red pencil line on the pages of the atlas. Maggie is a quick learner: she can recite the name of each port on their route. One night, Wallace awakes to find the cabin flooded with light. Framed in the porthole, a full moon hangs low in the sky, a bright pathway streaming down the rippling waves towards him.

'Margaret,' he whispers, 'look at the moon.'

Sleepily she turns towards him. Her eyes are huge when she wakes to the strange radiance gleaming on her skin. She murmurs, stretching her arms above her head and arching her back, inviting him. Gently he pulls her nightdress over her head and now there is nothing between them. Breast on bone. Breath on cheek. Skin on skin. He gathers her close to him, kisses her hard on her open mouth as they roll together in the bed. *The children* ... she gurgles with laughter, but no one hears them. They are in a private world, her hand on his thigh, creeping in to take hold of him, stiff and full. *Turn over*, he mouths, and she complies, crouching face down on the bed while he rises over her. The bony knobs of her spine, pale and smooth, like carved marble, in contrast to the moon-roundness of her buttocks, firm in his hands. With a groan, he enters her, just in time.

'The children,' she says, collapsing into the pillow.

In the argent light they lie awake, with arms, legs and fingers entwined until the moon goes down. When they are lulled to sleep, he dreams of a baby boy, named Wallace, after his father.

At Alexandria, a crowd of Arab pedlars swarms on board, selling trinkets, shells, lace, photographs, cigarettes, dates, coral, jewellery.

'Get you on!' Margaret shouts at a pedlar who comes near but he pays no heed. She lifts her parasol. The man dances out of range, waving his strings of beads and feathers. Furious, she is ready for the chase.

'God save us,' Wallace bounds towards her. 'But that wee man doesn't know the danger he's in.'

'Well, he is asking for it.'

'My companion in arms,' he murmurs, 'let's go and have tea.'

She leans on his arm. How patient he is, she thinks, how good-natured. Companions in arms, yes, they will face the future together. For better and for worse.

As the days grow hotter, the games room becomes a refuge. A long low room with a row of portholes along one wall, it is furnished with dark bentwood tables and chairs. Gathering together to play cards gives the passengers a purpose. Margaret has found a young girl to mind the children each day for a small payment, and Mr and Mrs Caldwell, the couple from Larne, have taught them how to play bridge. By the time they reach Port Said, Wallace and Margaret have fallen into a routine: spending their time indoors during the day and coming on deck only in the cool of the evening.

When the ship enters the Suez Canal, Wallace loses all interest in cards. He sits on a chair on deck, as the ship, its engines dulled, moves ahead. On either side, the banks are green and then desert, with lines of date palms. The water is so clear, he can see hundreds of jellyfish, in shades of blue. At narrow points of the canal the ship slows. In the stillness, the contrast between the desert, trees and water is everything. He remains out on deck, despite the sun's glare. Occasionally there is movement: a distant camel gliding along a ridge or a flotilla of dhows passing. Wallace is mesmerised by the canal itself: the intellectual daring, the scale, the enormity of effort behind its construction.

A shadow startles him. It is Mr Caldwell, dressed in a baggy cotton suit and white panama hat. Despite his bluff manner, there is an air of defeat about Mr Caldwell, in the lumbering shoulders, the red veins patterning his cheeks, the wobbling chins. The older man sinks into a chair beside Wallace.

Richard Caldwell has confided in Wallace that he works as a civil servant and has heart trouble. He baulked at the prospect of being sent back to India to assist in the relocation of the capital from Calcutta to Delhi. I told them, he said to Wallace: with my ticker, I'll kick the bucket on the job, but the blighters wouldn't listen.

'Damn heat.' He draws a silver case out of his pocket and removes a cigarette. As he smokes the two men sit and gaze out at the canal.

'What a remarkable feat of construction.'

No reply.

Undeterred, Wallace continues, 'Napoleon said it couldn't be done. He thought if the canal were dug here the Red Sea would drain into the Med. It took a French engineer to prove him wrong.'

His companion snorts. 'Took an Englishman to be the first man to bring a ship through. Ha, he knocked spots off those damn frogs. Admiralty man. Sailed in the dead of night without a light to guide him.'

Mr Caldwell is a staunch Unionist who has, in his own words, no time for the Liberals' twaddle about Home Rule. Wallace is too easy-going to argue.

Silence.

'Better go in,' Mr Caldwell says. 'The ladies will be waiting for us.'

Wallace is reluctant to abandon the sound of water slapping on the gunwale, the sunset turning gold, the passing life on the canal, but Mr Caldwell has taken the lead and is stamping down the stairs.

In the games room Margaret is sitting alone at a table.

'I'm sorry dear, to have kept you waiting.'

'Oh, I've only just arrived.'

At that moment Emily Caldwell appears, breathless with excitement. 'We saw the RMS Medina as clear as day, just before we entered the canal. It was far out but we saw it. Did you?'

She turns to Wallace who shakes his head, bemused.

'Oh, but you must have done,' she insists as she sits down and picks a card. 'I hear it's beautiful, with white livery and blue trim.'

Once Margaret has dealt, Mrs Caldwell picks up her cards without looking at them. She is a restless little woman with frizzy hair and a sharp nose. In Wallace's opinion, she talks far too much.

'What a pity you missed it. It's very famous. It was made into the royal yacht to carry King George and Queen Mary to India, along the very same route that we are on. Three years ago, I think. They were going to the Imperial Durbar in Delhi.'

'What is that?' Margaret asks.

'Why, it was the coronation ceremony. When the King was crowned Emperor of India.'

Margaret concentrates on the cards. 'I bid one no trump.'

Mrs Caldwell sighs. 'Oh, I would have so loved to have been there. The Imperial Durbar went on for over a week and the pomp and ceremony had to be *seen* to be believed. Thousands of people attended. The nabobs and princes on their elephants. The costumes, I believe, were simply magnificent. The King wore a crown made of every precious gem you could think of: diamonds, sapphires, emeralds and rubies. Just think!'

The others wait for her to bid but Mrs Caldwell is too absorbed to notice. 'There are eight arches in that crown I believe. It has six thousand, one hundred and seventy diamonds.'

'It's your bid, please, Mrs Caldwell,' Wallace says.

'Oops, silly me.' Bewildered, she stares at her cards as if she doesn't know how they came to be in her hand.

'Emily,' her husband barks, 'we are waiting.'

'Two hearts.' Delighted, she sits back in her chair, 'I get so carried away.'

Margaret stiffens. 'All that ostentation and fuss.'

'But it is our own King George, the dearest of men.'

'He is certainly the most *costly* of men.'

'Oh Margaret, you're making fun!'

'Not at all. I find the display of such wealth quite vulgar.'

'Oh!' Mrs Caldwell looks as if she is about to cry.

Seeing the colour rise in her husband's face, Wallace says quickly, 'Two no trump.'

'I pass,' says Mr Caldwell.

'Aha!' Margaret says with a flourish. 'Three no trump.'

She turns to Mrs Caldwell. 'We don't hold with monarchy, you see. It's all stuff and nonsense. Tom Paine had the measure of it. A hereditary king makes as much sense as a hereditary mathematician. As for an *emperor!*'

'Can't we just play cards?' Wallace implores.

Margaret takes a small black fan out of her purse to fan herself. Afterwards, she puts down the fan on the table, and pats her hair. 'Now,' she says brightly, 'where were we?'

Mr Caldwell's expression is murderous. 'I beg to differ with you, Mrs McKay.'

Wallace takes out his handkerchief to mop his forehead. 'The heat can make you feel fractious, don't you think?

No one says a word.

'The ship was taking such a long time getting through the canal I was quite glad,' he fibs, 'that Dick rescued me.'

Mr Caldwell stands up. 'I feel like an early night, Emily.'

'Do you, dear?' his wife says vaguely, engrossed in her cards.

'But you can't stop now!' Margaret exclaims. 'We've only just started the rubber.'

Mr Caldwell ignores her.

'Come on, old girl,' he orders. His wife protests but he pre-empts her by pulling out her chair while she is seated on it. He takes her shawl from the back of the chair and gives it to her.

His wife wrings her hands. 'But Dick, dear, I think we might win.'

'Gather your things, Emily, and be quick about it.'

'Well, I just don't know what.'

He turns and bows. 'I'll say good night to you, Mr and Mrs McKay.'

'Why, Mr Caldwell, you are leaving,' Margaret says archly, 'just when the contract is mine.'

Leaning close to her, Mr Caldwell hisses, 'Whether you win a hand or not, is immaterial to me. As a loyal Ulsterman, I will have no truck with Fenians and Papists.'

Margaret stands up, her chair crashing to the floor. The sound reverberates around the room like an explosion. There is an audible gasp from the other card players.

'For pity's sake, Margaret,' Wallace says.

Her voice is loud and ugly. 'I'll have you know that I'm as good a Protestant as you are.'

'The evidence of my own ears,' Mr Caldwell is puce with indignation. *'Stuff and nonsense ...'*

'Aye, I am a good Protestant,' Margaret says, 'and I am a true republican.'

Without a word, Mr Caldwell turns on his heel and stomps away. With a sigh, Emily Caldwell follows her husband out.

The next day when Wallace and Margaret enter the games room, they find the Caldwells already ensconced at another table.

'It does pay to be civil, dear,' Wallace reminds Margaret in the cabin later, but his caution seems only to make her worse. For the rest of the journey they find, more often than not, that they can't find partners to play with and are reduced to playing two-handed canasta. From then on, Margaret complains to Wallace about how many disagreeable people a body has to put up with on a sea voyage, and says the sooner they arrive in Calcutta the better it will be.

VI

INDIA 1914

Lay in a large stock of thin vests, Oxford shirts, socks, stockings and sturdy boots; but do not purchase white drill clothes in England – these can be obtained at one third of the cost in the bazaar at Calcutta.
– Advice to the tea planter going to Assam (1888)

As the ship negotiates its way between the sandbanks of the Hooghly river, Calcutta rises up out of the sea, against a backdrop of great white palaces decorated with bright green shutters. Soaring over the city, is the dome of the central post office.

When they land, Margaret is dazed by the sweltering heat, the thick dust, the roar of people and vehicles on the quayside. The Assam Company agent, Mr Johnson, who has come to meet them, guides the family through the crowds to a waiting cab. Wallace and Margaret climb in and sit in silence, while the trunks are loaded onto the roof. Mr Johnson is a white-suited, pink-faced young man with pale onion-coloured eyes who talks unremittingly.

'You'll be staying at the club. It has marvellous golf, you know, cricket too and there's a croquet lawn. Lots of amusement for the ladies. Better have some fun while you can.' The agent lets out a high, whinnying laugh. 'There will be nothing like it in Assam, I can tell you.'

He opens the window and shouts. The porters on the cab roof lean down into the window with their hands open.

'Greedy blighters,' Mr Johnson grumbles as he dispenses a handful of coins.

Margaret speaks only once, to Maggie when she climbs up on the seat to get a better view. 'Sit down, girl, this minute!'

What if the horse takes fright and the cab overturns into the dirt? She imagines strange, brown faces crowding in around her. The mere thought of it makes Margaret feel weak.

The streets are lined with the stalls of tradesmen: carpenters, silversmiths, sellers with weighing scales perched among piles of fruit and vegetables. People stream along the pavements: the men in loose garments and the women in saris. Such brilliance Margaret has never seen before: magenta, peacock blue, and iridescent shine against the crumbling, dung-coloured walls. She hears the unmelodic music of drums and tinkling bells from a Hindu temple, its columns decorated with mirrors and coloured stones. Painted statues, open-mouthed, display their flailing limbs.

Then, unexpectedly, everything changes: the streets become quiet, tree-lined and elegant. Formal gardens stretch out around a great, domed building.

'That is Queen Victoria's memorial,' Mr Johnson says.

Margaret sniffs.

Wallace smiles, 'I didn't expect to see such fine architecture.'

Mr Johnson looks lachrymose. 'Why they moved the capital from Calcutta to Delhi, I will never fathom.'

From behind an iron grille and trailing hibiscus of a balcony, two women gaze down at Margaret. Her attention is caught by the gold embroidery of their saris, the silver bangles on their brown arms, their thoughtful expressions.

'Here we are at last, safe and sound,' Mr Johnson exclaims as wrought iron gates open to receive them. The gates close behind them and the turbanned guards step back into position.

At the sight of the flowering gardens, the distant parkland, the majestic trees, the croquet lawn, Margaret relaxes. The Tollygunge Club is reassuringly English in atmosphere, if not in style: a long low timber building incorporating bedrooms with a veranda that overlooks the golf course.

'So far, so good,' Wallace smiles at her. A beetle crawls along the edge of his collar. She leans across and flicks it off with her glove. So far, so good, indeed. Despite the heat and the noise, the ramshackle streets, Margaret is light-headed with relief.

'It really is very *foreign!*' she whispers during their first dinner. Servants glide between the white tablecloths and shining glassware, a scent of incense in the air. Outside in the darkness, among the eucalyptus trees, the jackals cry like children.

Wallace smiles, 'What did you expect?'

That night, she falls asleep under a white canopy of mosquito netting and dreams of houses burning, wild animals chasing her through ruined streets as she runs, clutching her baby. In her dream she climbs to the highest point on the Queen Victoria memorial and at the top she finds an Indian man sitting cross-legged, his skinny arms and elongated fingers covered with jewels. Rubies. Emeralds. Diamonds. He snatches the screaming baby out of her arms and flings it away. Her heart thundering, Margaret wakes to the sound of the baby crying in the cot. *It's alright,* she mutters, as much to herself as to the baby. For a long time she rocks the cot. *Wallace,* she whispers but his back is a bulwark against her.

'I had an awful nightmare,' she says at breakfast. 'It must have been the egg pudding we had at dinner. It was too rich for someone like me who is used to plain fare.'

Wallace grunts, his head deep in the pages of *The Calcutta Times.*

Later they walk between the flowerbeds and onto the croquet lawn.

'Are there any snakes?' she wonders aloud, holding tight to the handle of her parasol.

'Bound to be.'

He is more adventurous, striding out each morning to the farthermost point on the estate, before returning for breakfast with tales of butterflies he's seen and a six-foot-long black snake that gave him a fright until one of the servants told him it was harmless.

'As long as this table it was,' he tells his daughter but she doesn't linger. Once she is free, the little girl goes looking to play with a thin, pale boy who sits with his father at breakfast each morning. Poor motherless thing, Margaret says, when she hears how the little boy lost his mother in a cholera epidemic of the previous year and how his father is bringing him home to England and a boarding school. At the bridge table the widower entertains them with stories of army life: the privations endured, the terrible food – horse meat, snake meat.

'Once,' he splutters with laughter, 'we lived on a diet of worms.'

'What about your wife?' Margaret wants to press him but she is cowed by the man's casual joviality. When they visit the Victoria Memorial, she does not say anything. Her dream is still too real. The imperial rule of law and order: all that stand between her and a teeming wildness. Thanks be, she says to Wallace and he looks hard at her to see if she's joking. Despite her unease, she can't get enough of the world in the streets. Every time they venture out, she trembles with excitement. Perspiration trickles down her cheeks and darkens her dress. She doesn't care. *Look, oh look, – may we stop to see?* Wallace is more reflective. He is thinking ahead to the next stage of the journey. Calcutta feels familiar to him, its wide streets and colonial architecture, the English ways of the Tollygunge: smoked kippers for breakfast and scones for afternoon tea. Beyond the city is mystery. On the map, the Brahmaputra river starts in the mountains and flows thousands of miles down to the coast.

They are making their preparations to leave Calcutta when the news comes through. The hotel guests gather in the morning room. They sit in little groups, drinking tea in china cups. The men in their white suits and the women, languorous, trailing silk and lace, are in a sea of anxious speculation.

'What does it mean?' Margaret wonders.

Wallace shrugs. 'I don't know what good it can do. The Kaiser is hell bent, apparently. He is causing havoc in Belgium and France, I believe. Thankfully the newspapers say the whole business will be over by Christmas.'

'I don't understand. Belgium and France! What have they to do with us?'

Wallace picks up the newspaper and reads aloud. 'The Prime Minister said in the House of Commons. "We are fighting to vindicate the principle that small nationalities are not to be crushed in defiance of international good faith by the arbitrary will of a strong and overmastering power."'

Margaret rests her chin on her hands. She doesn't notice her napkin sliding off her lap to drift onto the floor. A servant runs forward and crouches down to lift it up from under the table. He is about to drape the napkin onto her lap again when she waves him away loftily, saying, 'Get me another one.'

She turns to her husband. 'Do you know what I think?'

He steeples his fingers. 'Margaret, I know exactly what you think, but I'm afraid when Mr Asquith made his announcement he did not have our small nation in mind.'

'Well, he should have.'

'Yes,' Wallace said, 'you are absolutely right.'

And Margaret feels absurdly pleased.

She doesn't know which was worse, the river journey or what follows after. They disembark at a jetty beside a disconsolate row of reed huts. A queue of tongas and their drivers are lined up, waiting. It takes an age to lift the trunks from the steamer into small wooden boats and then transfer them onto oxen carts. By the time they start to move into the forest, the sun is at its height. Their progress so slow that Margaret wants to scream; at the discomfort of sitting on hard board seats, the torpor of the animals, the drivers swatting desultorily. This is a test of my spirit, she tells herself. Swathed in netting, she and the girls are safe from mosquitos. Little Maggie falls asleep and baby Elizabeth is quiet in her basket. Wallace sits upright, his face grim under his topee, his hand scrabbling at his collar.

'Darling, they're eating you alive.' Her gloved hand raises the corner of the net around her wide hat. 'Sit in close to me.'

He frowns but she insists. 'There's no one can see us here, for heaven's sake!'

He slides across the seat to her. Lifting her arms, she extends the netting around his head and shoulders and lets it fall.

'There now, isn't that better?' she murmurs. 'Now we are companions in arms.'

The two of them squashed together, encased in a mesh of light and shadow. The smells of her, the heat of her clothing: the sudden shock of intimacy. He slams against her as the pony goes over rough ground.

She giggles. 'Easy on!'

'You are one brave woman, Margaret,' he says, his hand closing on hers.

It is dark by the time they arrive at the tea garden at Mackeypore, and the gates open to receive them into a compound of bungalows. Monkeys chatter in the trees along the midnight driveway. Wakening from a doze, she is reminded of swallows in the eaves of the old farmhouse. An incongruous thought. It is bewildering: to travel halfway across the world and to be met by a landfall of memories. The house is a bungalow built on a platform. It has a deep veranda shaded by a steep reeded roof. Steps lead up to the wooden doors. The walls are made of uprights and cross-beams, and filled with panels of coarse jungle grass twisted together. In front of the steps the servants are lined up: the men in neat white clothes and the women with veiled heads. After the long journey up the reaches of the Brahmaputra river, the little family has finally arrived, hot and exhausted, at their destination.

'Welcome to our new home,' Wallace says.

For the first time since they left Ireland Margaret feels the tug of homesickness. She must not cry, not now. Forcing a laugh, she takes her daughter's hand and they alight from the tonga, stiff and sore.

'I see you've brought me all this way to live in a thatched house. For that I could have stayed at home.'

For a moment, Wallace looks abashed.

In the hall of the bungalow stand two native women, small and strong-boned. One of them opens her arms to little Maggie who is suddenly shy and hides in her mother's skirts, while Elizabeth, the baby, is swept up in the other's embrace. It is not surprising that Margaret is reminded of Ballygowan: the bungalow has a homely, rustic quality, the deep veranda, the rooms opening up with a startled air as if someone has just slipped away through a secret door. In the dining room, places are set with fine bone china and glass goblets. That is a pretty sight, she thinks, and a cut above anything she has ever seen in Ballygowan.

By the end of the week there are still trunks piled up waiting to be unpacked. Margaret stands in the middle of the bedroom while the women glide around her. The silence is broken only by the sound of monkeys scrabbling in the thatch and the slap of bare feet on the wooden floor. Once finished their tasks, the women come back to stand beside her. In a wordless exchange, Margaret lifts garments out of the trunk and hands them on. Embroidered petticoats and pillowcases pass from her pale fingers into theirs, small and dark, on the white linen.

The gloom of the bedroom, the bed prominent on the wooden floor, the carved chairs and dressing table, feel familiar. The rain hammering on the windows and the smell of damp timber pull her back to the old farmhouse on a summer's day: her sisters playing under an Irish sky, banked high with clouds, louring over the fields. Concentrate on something real, Margaret tells herself, on something small and old. She lifts out a linen table runner from the trunk and lets it slide through her fingers. The ridges of embroidery distinct on her thumbs. The painstaking stitches. Every petal and stem, the curlicues in each corner.

Yes, she thinks, I'll write to my sister Molly at once, after the unpacking is done, and I'll tell her all my news. She is conscious of the presence of others in the room: the two small figures who shadow her at every turn. She lifts a pile of folded sheets out of the trunk.

'Put them in the armoire.' She points to the carved wardrobe towering in the corner. *Armoire* she laughs aloud. Since when has she got such airs? There are, as Wallace promised, a lot of servants.

'They take up so much of my time,' she writes to Molly with a certain pride.

> I have to tell them everything at least twice and they just smile. I can't tell what they're saying and they seem to find difficulty understanding me. There are two ayahs, one to mind Maggie, one to mind little Elizabeth, and, soon, I'll have another one for the new baby. The cook is a fat Mussulman with a liking for drink, although it is against his religion. He reminds me a bit of Uncle Adam. Don't you remember how his head was scrambled with drink at times? Every morning, I call this fellow in and tell him about the meals I want him to cook, but more often than not, it's all in one ear and out the other. The pantomime ends with me shouting and he doing exactly what he wants. Dear Molly, that's only the start of it. There are so many servants: a bearer, an assistant to the cook, two *pani-wallahs* to carry water, one sweeper called a *mater*, two *chowkeydars* (watchmen), two *punkah-wallahs*, a *syce* for the horse, two *malee* (gardeners), a *moorgie-wallah*, who looks after the chickens, and a *gorukhiya* (the cow-herd). And not a bell to be had in the bungalow. I have to yell each time I need a servant. I sound like a street hawker.

The long and tedious journey upriver failed to dampen her spirits: she felt she was a missionary travelling into the darkest jungle, but once they are settled at Mackeypore, it isn't long before boredom sets in. Another letter ribbons in her head.

Dear Molly, the girls are in seventh heaven. There are monkeys everywhere and we have to employ small boys to throw stones at them. Everyone was standing on the steps of the veranda to welcome us when we arrived. The Frobishers and Alistair, the only white faces among them. Mr and Mrs Frobisher are nice people in their own way. Not learned in any way. I'd say neither of them ever opened a book but it was sweet the way she came forward to see the baby. The Frobishers don't have any children and you can see, just by the way the wife trails after Maggie, that she would like to have one of her own. Alistair is a young man, fresh out from England and utterly miserable from the look of him. He is scarcely twenty years old and has the air of someone who has lost his way. Mrs Frobisher is quite imposing. She was born out here in the mountains. She is the daughter of an army officer while Mr Frobisher is quite common. He came out from England as a tea planter. From the look of him there is a touch of the tar brush, I'd say, but of course I don't say. The Frobishers are opposites in every way. He is short, curly-haired and plump, while Mrs Frobisher is remarkably thin, angular, with a worried expression. She talks the King's English in such a plummy accent that I want to laugh out loud. He is a plain-speaking Yorkshire man with manners to match. It's hard to see how they ever got together but I suppose, in this part of the world, you don't have much choice ...

'Oh, my dear, we are so glad you have arrived safely. So glad,' Mrs Frobisher says, 'but, I regret to say, we are just ships passing in the night. My time is short.'

Margaret takes her outstretched hand and wonders: is the woman dying? It turns out that Mrs Frobisher is not dying. She is delicate, and is going to spend six months in Shillong, a hill station in the Khasi hills where the air is dry and healthy.

'I cannot abide to spend a minute longer here. The lowland does not suit my disposition.'

Margaret clucks sympathetically.

'Watch out for the mosquitos, my dearest,' Mrs Frobisher says as she walks away. 'Big as mice, they eat you alive.'

'Dear Molly,' Margaret eventually writes:

I can describe the place we are in now. Row upon row of tea plants stretch out in the shade of acacia trees. You should see the tea pluckers work. Native women with baskets on their backs and the quickest hands you've ever seen. Wallace is a giant among them, a true Brobdingnagian and twice as awkward. And yet I have not seen him so happy, not even on our wedding day. He has his tea-tasting operation and enjoys being in charge, I think. We have settled in quite well. Wallace spends his time in the tea factory and I spend much of my time reading in bed these days. In my condition it makes sense to stay out of the heat. I am feeling very strong, despite the climate and the food. Wallace does the worrying for the two of us. Sometimes I am *Alice in Wonderland*: the butterflies here are enormous, the colours of the flowers indescribable, such gorgeous lilies and orchids. As soon as they are cut and put in vases around the house they shrivel up, leaving a disgusting smell. The nights are filled with noise, bats, flying foxes and owls. Such bawling in the forest, that, at times, it is difficult to sleep. I pine for a bit of soft Irish rain and a big dish of boxty. I never stop eating. I seem to be getting bigger by the day. This baby will be a whopper. We went to the polo club. It is the only amusement here but I'm too far gone now. It's mainly men, tea planters of course. A few wives I've got to know but we live so far apart and the club is our only meeting place. People drink such a lot that I'm surprised the gin doesn't come out of their pores. The only woman here in the tea garden is Mrs Frobisher. She comes to visit me most days. The children are fond of her and I've grown used to her theatrical manner. She fans herself constantly with an enormous feather fan and says things like, "If I don't get away soon, my darling, I will simply fall away to nothing." My dear Molly, please write soon. I need cheering up. Your loving sister, Margaret.

By the time Mrs Frobisher leaves for Shillong, she is sunken-eyed and gaunt. A tonga has been filled with cushions and blankets to ease her journey. She lies back, murmuring so weakly that Margaret had to lean in to hear.

'Sorry to abandon you when you're so close to your time.' A whisper of a smile. 'Not that I'm much help. Mrs Brewster will see you right and little Maggie's ayah, Baia, will help you. She asked to come with me, did I tell you? Baia is from Shillong, but I told her that she must stay and assist you in your hour of need.'

Thank you for nothing, Margaret thinks. Baia is my ayah, not yours.

'Goodbye, my darling,' Mrs Frobisher says, extending her hand. A bird's claw, Margaret thinks, has more flesh on it. She peers into the woman's face; at the blue vein on her temple; the bruised eyelids. On her cheek, the woman's breath is shallow.

'Isn't your husband coming to say goodbye?'

Mrs Frobisher falls back in the cushions, a faint look of disdain on her face. Mr Frobisher, apparently, has already gone to the tea factory to meet Wallace. The young man, Alistair is nowhere to be seen. There is no one else to say goodbye to Mrs Frobisher, so Margaret, the children and their ayahs stand at the gate, waving until the tonga disappears among the trees.

I am the only woman left on the estate, Margaret thinks as she walks back to the bungalow. She feels the baby kick inside her, alerting her to the enormity of her isolation. There is Wallace, but he is stuck in his work. She wants to do something ... anything: to use her hands to play the piano, paint a watercolour, to recall a culture that exists beyond the dense greenery of forest, the secret animal tracks.

Occasionally she visits the tea gardens and the factory, but mostly spends her time in the drawing room of the bungalow where the only sounds are of the singing bird in its cage and her two little girls chattering. Am I afraid, she wonders, that one day, like Mrs Frobisher, I will disappear?

'I'm sleeping my life away,' she grumbles to Wallace over dinner.

Silence.

'Maybe, this time,' she dares to hope, 'it will be a little boy.'

His eyes give nothing away.

'You look tired.'

Wallace grimaces. 'Good enough is never good enough for Mr Frobisher.'

After dinner they go into the drawing room and sink into two deep leather armchairs, their silence broken only by the girls running in to say good night. The ayahs are ever watchful, the children leave the room as quickly as they had come, a void pooling behind them. Idly Margaret peruses the bookshelves. The previous occupant of the bungalow left books in all the rooms. His particular interest was the Crimean War. One book is entitled *Travels and Adventures in the Province of Assam, during a residence of fourteen years.*

Fourteen years! A living death. She must keep herself busy. There are letters to write. One day she writes:

Dear Molly, I'm getting heavier every day and the heat is killing me. The day of my confinement can't come quick enough, believe me. Mrs Brewster will be with me, I'm glad to say. She is a midwife and a nurse, who is very obliging. She lives in Tezpur, a good fifty miles away but she has promised she will be here in time. She visited us once already, to check on my condition. She made the journey up through the hills in jig time. She is an enormously fat, red-faced lady who rides a poor, spavined horse and wears men's jodhpurs and a topee. Such a commotion she made when she arrived, ordering the servants to lift her down off the horse, that I thought we were under attack from savages. When I came out of the house she was dismounting with the help of four servants who were in kinks of laughter while she was cursing disgracefully. I'd never heard such language. By the time she was down, the servants were in hysterics and she took her whip to them. I liked her immediately. She was in no hurry to leave and took afternoon tea in the drawing room with me and was happy to meet Wallace when he returned from the factory. It was dark by the time she had finished dining with us. She drank whiskey (our little store of Bushmills is reducing fast) and told us hair-raising stories about the fate of tea planters she had known who had fallen into the hands of tribal warriors. I was astonished when she refused to stay the night. Wouldn't hear of it, she said. There was a foal back in Tezpur that needed her attention.

On the day Margaret goes into labour, Mr Frobisher insists that Wallace join him and Alistair for dinner. Wallace demurs but Mr Frobisher is unbending.

'Sundowners at six. Dinner at seven,' he says, his face stiff with embarrassment.

Margaret's labour has started mid-morning. Wallace comes back from the tea factory and spends the afternoon in a welter of anxiety, until Mrs Brewster arrives.

'How glad I am,' he stammers. She brushes past him, goes in and slams the bedroom door behind her. The muffled cries bring him back to Seacon, to the ugly sounds of a calving cow. He slips out to the veranda and stands, rigid as a whippet, gripping the rail. What was he thinking of, to bring Margaret to this godforsaken place? Every day is filled with danger: malaria, meningitis, diphtheria, yellow fever. The polo club echoing with stories of tragedy: a dog gone rabid, a baby born dead, a man poleaxed by fever.

He escapes out into the darkness. A man has to eat, after all. The Frobishers' bungalow is a grander version of their own, with a delicately crafted veranda rail running along the facade. Lamps are ablaze in every window.

'You'll have a peg,' Mr Frobisher says.

'Thank you, but I don't drink,' Wallace says, not for the first time. His companion continually tries to get him to take a drink.

'Suit yourself.' Head down into his collar, Mr Frobisher glowers at one end of the table, nursing a large whiskey, mutton stew congealing on the plate before him. Wallace sits at the other end. The young man Alistair sits beside him. The oil lamp in the centre of the table throws their faces into shadow. We could be holed up in a cave, Wallace thinks. Without finishing his dinner, Alistair asks to be excused. Wallace looks on with envy as the young man slips out of the room.

The conversation between the two men is desultory, mainly about matters to do with the tea garden. Mr Frobisher is in a bad mood.

'The company want us to up our production, but I can't see how we can. Damn labourers haven't it in 'em.'

Wallace, chewing on a piece of gristle, says nothing.

'You're new, of course,' Mr Frobisher continues. 'The biggest trouble we have is getting labour. The natives won't work in tea, so we depend on bringing 'em in from wherever we can find. And then, after we go to all that trouble, they get sick from cholera and die, and we have to send our *jouti* out hunting for more.'

'I see,' Wallace says.

'Or else they scarper. Disappear into the jungle.'

A servant removes their half-eaten plates of stew and replaces them with small bowls of blancmange. Mr Frobisher eats noisily. Wallace racks his brains for something to say. He has no dealings with the pluckers, whom he sees on his way to the factory, standing in little knots under the acacia trees. Each day he passes the line where the labourers live, with their naked children and bony dogs.

'Could they be paid a little more, maybe, to encourage them?'

'Definitely not!'

Wallace is nonplussed.

'We used Chinese workers here once upon a time.'

'Really?'

Mr Frobisher gazes at the wall. Lord, Wallace thinks, what a hard man he is to converse with. There is no give in him at all. He settles the spoon in his dish with a sigh. A bit more pudding wouldn't have gone astray.

Suddenly his host guffaws, wipes his mouth and says. 'Went on strike once. There was a terrible kerfuffle but we showed them who is boss.' His mirth is startlingly brief. 'Aye, they paid dearly. One planter cut the ears off any labourer who tried to run away.'

'Good Lord!' Nervously Wallace wipes his hands in his napkin.

By now Mr Frobisher's face is an unhealthy purple colour. Sweat glistens on his forehead.

'Poor bloody blighter, ' he says hoarsely.

Wallace is grateful that his host, despite his rough manner, has some fellow feeling towards his labourers. A good Yorkshire man at heart.

'Most unfortunate,' Wallace agrees.

'What that man had to suffer. He ended up in court. Some fanatic Quaker ladies back in England got wind of it. Ha!'

Mr Frobisher stares at Wallace, daring him to disagree. Blowing his cheeks out as if to caution him. 'Thankfully the judge was a good egg. Threw the case out.'

Wallace feels his jaw tighten. This is what happens when men go abroad. They end up pukka sahibs and lose any sense of right and wrong. The Quakers who educated me, he wants to say, were anything but fanatical. His desire to speak is tempered by his natural inclination to avoid a row. 'Maybe, the company could employ some more labourers.'

Mr Frobisher balls up his napkin and throws it on the table. 'Damn stupidity!'

He pours himself another whiskey, leans back in his chair and closes his eyes. Dinner is over and so, it is clear, is their conversation.

That night Wallace sits under the thatched roof of the veranda until he is forced indoors by a deluge of raindrops bouncing off the wooden rails. Inside the drawing room the air is charged with a strange energy. He tries to sleep in his armchair, blocking out the sounds from the bedroom. Day is dawning when the midwife comes out of the bedroom. Briskly cheerful, she informs Wallace that the infant is a girl who has two legs, two arms and a fine pair of lungs. The rain drums on the roof and streams down the windows. In the grey light, Wallace is drowning with fatigue.

'You can come in now, Mr McKay.'

Up close Mrs Brewster's round face is still flushed with exertion. There is a look of fierce pride in her eyes. Together the women have wrestled new life into the world while he cowered out on the veranda. A particularly female triumph, he thinks, crowned by the fact that the baby is a girl. Mrs Brewster brushes past him to pat the sheets and plump the pillows under Margaret's whey-coloured face and tangled hair. His wife gives Wallace a hazy, mindless smile. Beside her the baby lies in a cradle, asleep. He bends to kiss his wife's forehead. Her skin is cold and damp. He is powerless in the light of what she has endured, and yet resentment flickers at the thought: *Another girl* ... What goes into the mix to guarantee a son? Both their genetic lines are well-set: there are boys in Margaret's family and, in his own family, his brothers and himself. Science has no answer. Margaret and he might go on producing daughters for ever. He is overcome with shame. Holding her close is easier than looking into her eyes.

'My dearest,' he whispers, folding her in his arms. 'My sweet, what you've been through I can only imagine.'

Sighing deeply, she lies back in the pillows. 'She looks like you.'

He leans over the cradle and examines the baby's face under her frilled bonnet. The baby's eyes snap open. He is caught in the cold blue of her stare.

'I want to call her Alexandra,' Margaret says. 'What do you think?'

He thinks that the coverlet on the bed looks soft and inviting. His desire to sleep is overwhelming. He wants to unlace his boots, stretch out, fully clothed, beside his wife and close his eyes.

Mrs Brewster gives a warning cough. 'Mrs McKay needs to rest.'

Wallace knows better than to argue. He kisses his wife's forehead again and, seeing entreaty in her eyes, bends over the cradle. The baby's skin is warm and smells vaguely of carbolic soap.

'That is a very big name for a wee wean,' is all he says.

In the mornings, Margaret gives the two older girls their lessons in simple arithmetic and reading. In the afternoons she lies down for a nap. When the temperature has cooled, she sits on the veranda and writes letters or reads any book she can find. There is nothing else for her to do. Even the baby is growing fast and doesn't need her as much. Day follows day without mercy. She has become a ghost, seen and yet unseen. In an effort to shake off her torpor, she decides to walk every day to the perimeter of the tea garden. A good discipline if nothing else.

The tea pluckers don't look up when she walks along the track shaded by acacias. She has grown accustomed to the sight of the women in their robes, splodges of white in the greenery. Around their heads a cloth band holds the basket, freeing their fingers to flick up the leaves. She savours the calm, ordered scene. Work has a shape, she thinks, with a beginning and an end. It has a position, a purpose.

On one occasion, her heart beats in her throat when a brown bear passes near her and lopes off into the forest. I am invisible, she thinks, even to the animals. She visits Wallace in his office and finds him peering through a microscope. A sample of tea is boiling on a small fire. He professes to be pleased to see her, even offers her a cup of tea, but his abstracted air tells her otherwise. There is no place for her in the roaring heat of rolling machines and squealing engines. She inspects – from a distance – the living quarters of the labourers. She knows nothing about the men and women who work in the tea garden. Mrs Frobisher told her that a shortage of workers in Assam means that hundreds of labourers have been brought from Calcutta. They are housed in the line of timber huts at the furthest edge on the plantation.

'Labourers have to be kidnapped,' Mrs Frobisher told her once. 'Otherwise none of them would ever come here.'

'Was she joking? Margaret was too much in awe of her hostess to ask. She asks Wallace. 'What did she mean, *kidnapped*?'

He shrugs.

On Sundays there is no work to be done except for firing in the tea house. Some of the labourers get drunk on rum shrub and dance and sing into the night. The sounds carry in the air to where she and Wallace sit after dinner on the veranda. They can hear the drumming of tom-toms, the wailing of voices. Wallace taps his fingers on the table. 'If they keep this up, there'll be precious little work done in the morning.'

The noise continues, unabated. He rams his hands into his pockets.

Those people are exiles, Margaret thinks, and they are far from home.

'How mournful their celebrations are!' she says.

With nothing useful for me to do she asks herself: is it any wonder that I spy on the labourers? Life in the line seems simple, almost carefree: the brown-skinned men in their white loin cloths and loose turbans, the women in robes, the naked children. She decided to put her time to good use. Armed with a pencil and a sketch pad, she begins to sketch what she sees: the clusters of women, the children playing in the dust. Sometime in the future she might even hold a little exhibition of her sketches in the polo club. *Scenes from an Assamese tea garden.*

One morning she arrives earlier than usual. The line is empty. The gong will not sound for a half an hour or so. A morning fog has lifted off the hills and the air is deathly still. Even the birds are silent. A butterfly trembles on a leaf at her elbow. She holds her breath. Could I sketch it, she wonders, without frightening it away?

Then she sees the man lying on the ground.

It is very strange for a labourer to sleep while all the others are at work. There is something strange too, about the way the man lies with his head flung back. Curiosity wins out over caution and, still hidden in the trees,

Margaret comes nearer. Flies buzz around the man's head. She can see ants crawling along the bloody lacerations on his torso. One eye stares up at the sky, the other eye is hidden in a swollen mass of flesh. A woman is crouched beside him. On seeing Margaret, the woman jumps up and disappears into a hut.

Margaret is unable to move. There must be something she can do. In the next moment, the sound of the gong, beating madly in the air, shocks her into realising that the labourers are returning to the line. She hurries back along the path until, at a safe distance, she looks back and sees that the woman is again crouching beside the mutilated body.

In the bungalow her daughters are waiting for her. They dance around her with news that a cobra has been found on the veranda and that the ayah, Baia has taken it away on a stick and let it go free in the forest. Margaret is barely able to take in what they're saying. *A cobra on the veranda.* In this cursed country, she wondered, is anywhere safe? She puts her sketch pad into the mahogany cabinet and leans her head against the glass doors. Is she going to faint? One thing she knows: there will be no exhibition of her sketches in the polo club.

'Mummy is not well,' she says to the little girls before going into the darkened bedroom. Wide awake, she lies on the bed and stares at the ceiling. There is nothing she could have done, she whispers. Nothing at all.

That evening, at dinner, she tells Wallace where she has been.

'Good God, Margaret. The line is no place for a lady.'

She is unusually meek. 'Yes, Wallace.'

'You must promise me that you will never go there again.'

'I'll give you my word, but only if you tell me what happened.'

He shakes his head. 'It is none of your business, Margaret.'

'Please tell me,' she says softly. ' Or I will worry.'

And so he tells her. Feuds among the labourers are common enough. As usual, he said, one of their leaders came to ask Frobisher to parley between two labourers who were causing trouble.

'What happened?'

'Instead of making peace, Frobisher ordered them to fight it out. The dangerous foolishness of the man. They fought so hard, the other labourers begged the sahib to put a stop to it.'

He falls silent, chewing on his lip.

'Please go on.'

He takes a deep breath. 'By then, Frobisher had taken a bet on one of them. He even forced young Alistair to bet against him. The two men fought to the death for a bet.'

'Oh, my dear Lord, what was he thinking?'

Without warning, Wallace slams his fist on the table. 'Frobisher doesn't think. Now we are one man down, he'll have to shell out for a new labourer *and* get him trained.'

She feels a stab of fear. Wallace McKay is a man of quiet composure who, even under provocation, does not, as a rule, raise his voice. She is the one with a temper, who lets fly, and sometimes, she has to admit, for no good reason. She looks up to Wallace and depends on him to keep their life on an even keel. And now the memory of the native woman crouching in the dust has come between them. What was her mother's favourite saying?

'We are all Adam's children,' she says.

'Malcolm Frobisher isn't. He is a monster.'

'Oh, my dear,' she reaches out and clasps his hand. 'I meant the labourer.'

During the monsoon season, everything conspires against her. The rain thundering on the thatch roof gives her a headache. The sounds of the children, confined indoors and running about in a state of excitement add to her misery.

'I can't hear myself think.'

Six pairs of startled eyes gaze at her: three little girls and their ayahs.

The racket you're making,' she says to them.

As soon as the rain stops, she sends them out to walk as far as they can before the next deluge. Then she has time to sit on the veranda and gather her thoughts, but there is never enough time before the girls return, screaming with laughter and soaked to the skin from a fresh downpour.

The bedroom becomes her refuge. It is hot and stuffy but it is the only place she can be on her own. How is it that a body can feel lonely and yet never be alone? Her privacy is short-lived: the children seek her out, or the servants come looking for instructions. She has nothing onerous to do and yet every intrusion fills her with resentment. The evenings are no better. It is unnerving to sit at the big table with the servants creeping around her as she waits for Wallace to come back from the tea factory. When he does appear, he is preoccupied and so tired he can barely eat. Once dinner is over, he falls asleep, as if by clockwork, in his armchair in the drawing room.

There are times, Margaret writes in a letter to her sister that she never sends because she is ashamed of her own weakness, when I wonder if we are already dead: Wallace flat out in his armchair and me, entombed within the four walls of this house.

When she receives a letter from Mrs Frobisher, it is a sign that anything can happen. Mrs Frobisher has risen, Lazarus-like, from the dead or, at least, from the likelihood of death.

'Life here, in Shillong is very pleasant, dear Margaret, you would love it.' Mrs Frobisher writes in her cursive scrawl.

We have parties and theatricals too. Ladies are in demand here as the men greatly outnumber us. There are a few of the old regiment based in town. One of the officers plays the piano for dances in the Club and we have bridge parties in each other's houses. I have a fine house and garden. Only three servants unfortunately but I make do. I am afraid I have to close now. I have so much to tell you but I must fly or I'll be late for tiffin at the club.
Your friend Lavinia Frobisher.
PS. Please tell my husband, if he asks, that I am not well and that I spend my days in bed. Of course, I can tell *you* the truth: I have never felt better. The climate here is so congenial and, darling (*Mrs Frobisher has underlined three times*), there are no mosquitoes.

Reading the letter, Margaret is consumed with a sudden rage. She crushes the paper in her hand. How dare that woman be happy! In the mirror above the table, she barely recognises the sallow, heavy face staring back at her. She has grown to hate her life: the sweltering heat, punctuated by torrents of rain; her daily conversation shrunk to the level of three small children; the ennui of long, empty afternoons.

'Mrs Frobisher managed to escape,' she rails at her reflection, 'so why can't I?'

As a diversion, Wallace brings her for an evening at the polo club. The club is fifteen miles away and the journey on horseback is possible only when there is a full moon to light their way home. The clubhouse overlooks a polo ground. It is immaculately maintained despite the fact that neither of them has ever seen anyone play polo. On their arrival, they find the usual circle of tea planters drinking quantities of whisky and gin. Wallace's abstemiousness is viewed with a barely-disguised contempt by the men who make him welcome. There are a few wives for Margaret to talk to and, to her annoyance, none of them play bridge. After their pleasantries are exhausted, she goes out on the veranda and stands, frowning into the night.

'Darling, come and sit down beside me.' Wallace is half out of his seat and pointing to an empty space beside him on the couch and so she ends up squashed between her husband and Mr Frobisher whom, she realises too late, is very drunk.

'This lady,' Mr Frobisher insists loudly, 'is a little wifey from old Ireland with so many children she doesn't know what to do.'

Through the silk material of her dress, she feels his hand, hot and damp, on her knee. She shrinks away, tugging at her husband's arm, but Wallace is deep in conversation about tea prices on the English market with a deaf tea planter sitting on his other side. Undeterred, Mr Frobisher's hand delves deeper as, mewling softly, he pushes up against her. There is a thread of tobacco juice on his chin.

Quelling an urge to scream, Margaret pushes him away with all her strength. With a groan, Mr Frobisher slumps back and closes his eyes. Better not to make a fuss, she decides. Her husband, after all, has to answer to this man and Mr Frobisher has been without his wife for eight months. Is it any wonder he drinks too much? Then she remembers the cruel bet and decides that he is a dangerous, disgusting man and she doesn't blame Lavinia one bit for getting away from him.

Later, in the darkness of their bedroom, she shrinks from her husband's touch. She is so sorry, she wants to say, but she can't bear the thought of intimacy after the evening she's endured. In broken whispers, she tells him what happened at the polo club earlier that evening. When she is finished Wallace lies perfectly still.

'Did I do right?' She is anxious now, leaning up on her elbow to look at him. 'How I didn't lose my temper with him, I'll never know, but I didn't want to make a fuss. I mean his wife has gone away. The man is all alone.'

Wallace turns towards her. 'No, my dear,' he says. 'He is not alone.'

Puzzled, she waits for him to continue.

'Mr Frobisher took in the widow after the labourer was killed in that fight.'

She hears his words but there is only space in her mind for a man lying dead on the ground and a woman crouched by his side. 'I don't understand.'

'Must I spell it out?' his voice is harsh. 'Frobisher's taken the labourer's widow into his bed.'

That night, the unseen barrier which locked them in two separate worlds falls apart. It seems to Margaret that, for the first time since they arrived in India, each of them is free to articulate their deepest thoughts. She makes it clear that she can no longer stay in a place where Malcolm Frobisher, a man with no moral sense, holds sway. In turn, Wallace reveals that, for some time, he has wanted to leave the tea garden and set up as an independent agricultural inspector. He held back from confiding in her, he says, because there is always a risk that he might fail.

'Hush,' Margaret places her finger on his lips. 'We are companions in arms, remember?'

'Actually,' he says, 'I put out some feelers to the company and they are as keen as mustard.'

'There, I knew it,' she says triumphantly.

'And I agree the girls cannot continue to live here. A man like Frobisher is a degenerate.'

For a moment, silence, like an unexpected gift, envelops them. His breath is slow and even. Is he asleep?

'Wallace,' she whispers.

'I'm awake.'

'Where are we going to live?'

It turns out Wallace hasn't given any thought to where they might live.

'A typical man,' she teases. 'His career comes first, his wife and children left without a roof over their heads.'

She loves the sound of his laughter. How long it has been, she thinks, since we were so easy together. And then he asks her where she wants to live and she answers immediately. She wants to go up into the mountains, to the hill station of Shillong, where Mrs Frobisher is and where the air is healthy and the girls will have other children to play with and she won't be lonely all the time.

'If we can live there,' she says, swallowing a lump in her throat, 'I will be the happiest woman in India.'

He is thoughtful. 'I'll have to travel a fair bit but we do need to live somewhere. A hill station would be a good place for you and the children. I can see that. Shillong.'

In his mouth it sounds magical: a waterfall dropping from a great height. *Shillong.*

She has won.

Languidly she turns towards him, offering her mouth to his.

'I'll put it to the company,' he says, 'and see what they say.'

His hand burrows between her legs as they kiss. Dawn is streaking the sky when they fall asleep, curved together like silver spoons in a velvet-padded drawer.

VII

When Margaret hears that there was an old army sanatorium in Shillong she had a vision of Lavinia Frobisher propped up in bed in one of the wards, cheerily entertaining a gathering of army officers. Since her departure, as Mr Frobisher hasn't mentioned his wife, Margaret is never called upon to lie about the letter she received. She writes to Mrs Frobisher to tell her they are coming to Shillong and receives a letter in turn that began with the words: 'How wonderful it will be to see you again and your dear husband Jack.'

Wallace reads the first line, points out that the woman couldn't even get his name right and refuses to read any more.

On their journey, Margaret recounts to Wallace everything that Lavinia Frobisher has written. Shillong is in the Khasi hills, a hill town much favoured by regimental officers and their wives. It is known as *The Scotland of the East* on account of the beauty of its wooded highlands. Its climate is very bearable: winters resemble English weather: dry and cool, while summers are wet. It has a new nine-hole golf course and a wonderful social club. Unlike many of the buildings in Shillong which were damaged in an earthquake twelve years earlier, the golf course has survived intact. In particular, Mrs Frobisher wants Margaret to know, there is a track used for horse races.

As they travel higher into the hills the ponies slow their pace and the air cools. Wallace and Margaret and the children wrap themselves in rugs and shawls and huddle together to keep warm.

'This really is a fresh start for us,' she says.

His expression is lugubrious. 'Are you sure you'll be alright settling in?'

'Of course, I will.'

'You know that I'll be travelling a great deal.'

'You keep telling me that. We will have to manage somehow, won't we girls?'

'Yes, Mummy,' they chorus with delight.

'I might even take up golf.'

Wallace is offended. 'Golf is a game for men.'

She smiles. 'And you are welcome to it.'

In Shillong they travel, at first, along noisy, busy streets crowded with people, smelling of horse dung and drains. The narrow streets plunge between dilapidated wooden buildings. Tiers of houses, one below the other, stagger down the hillsides, almost toppling into the river gorge. Then they come into the European quarter of the town where white women wear fashionable hats and woollen dresses under their coats and men sport tweed mufflers around their necks. As they pass the golf club, clusters of people stand on the veranda where afternoon tea is being served. The sharp, thin air makes Margaret feel light-headed. Soon she will be among people she can talk to. The smells of eucalyptus and pine are in her nostrils. Mist presses down on the secretive hills that seem to go on forever. The place really is like Scotland, or how she imagines Scotland to be.

At last, stiff and sore, they climb out of the tonga. It takes them a moment to get their bearings. Here is the road, here the garden gate, facing them the plaque on the wall. *Elderslie.*

'That's a Scottish name. Renfrewshire, I believe,' Wallace murmurs, but Margaret isn't listening. With bated breath, she opens the gate. At the sight of the bungalow with its white veranda, her spirits rise.

'No thatch!' she claps her hands. 'We have a real roof at last.'

It is the first time Wallace has seen her happy for a long time. Since Alexa's birth, a lethargy has weighed her down: days spent in the dispiriting gloom of their bedroom; in the evening, her sullen features facing him across the dinner table. His wife's delight is a relief. The little girls skitter around the veranda and in and out of the house. The baby chuckles and waves her hands. *This is what a home feels like ...* Margaret thinks as she moves from room to room. For the first time in a long time, her heart surges at the sight of the girls running towards her. She must always do the best for her daughters.

'Where will we sleep?' Maggie asks. That haughty look of hers will take her far, her mother thinks. Elizabeth, round-eyed, slips her chubby hand into her father's hand and gazes up at his great height. 'But, Daddy, where has my ayah gone?'

Theirs is a smaller household now, with fewer servants. Only the Khasi ayah, Baia, has travelled with them to Shillong. The new cook is well-mannered and even speaks a little English. Each morning Margaret gives him orders for the day and, to her surprise, he follows her instructions. The house is easy to manage: three bedrooms, the kitchen and Wallace's office beside the main central living room which has a large fireplace that Margaret insists must be cleaned out and set every morning. She likes to see a fire lighting in the grate.

Beyond the veranda, a garden surrounded by enormous trees slopes down to the road. Two gardeners tend the garden and a local woman keeps the bungalow clean.

'Everything is very satisfactory,' Margaret tells Mrs Frobisher when her friend accepts her invitation to join her for afternoon tea.

Resting her cup on the saucer, Lavinia Frobisher agrees. 'My dear Margaret, after what you've been through. I mean, the baby and everything.'

Margaret doesn't mention Mr Frobisher, and his wife doesn't ask about him. Every movement the other woman makes is laborious as if she finds the effort too much for her. All the same, it is a changed woman who is sitting on the edge of her chair sipping tea and consuming a large slice of madeira cake. Lavinia Frobisher was little more than skin and bone on the day she left for Shillong. Margaret wondered then if she would ever see her alive again. Now her guest displays the sleekness of an over-fed greyhound.

As if she can read Margaret's mind, Mrs Frobisher smiles. 'I had a terrible time getting here. I thought I would be dead by the time we made Shillong. At least there are horses now. In my grandmother's day a lady was carried in a basket strapped to a native's back. The discomfort was appalling and the natives were terribly slow.'

'Good heavens!'

'We have come up in the world,' Mrs Frobisher says as she brushes cake crumbs off her hands, 'both literally and figuratively.'

Yes, I have come a long way, Margaret thinks. From being a slip of a girl in Ballygowan to becoming a mother of three, with another on the way, and with a house and servants and a decent husband. Poor Lavinia Frobisher, for all her airs and graces, she has never felt the kick of an infant in her womb. Humiliating, if she knew her husband was having his way with a native woman at night.

'Another cup?'

'Lovely tea but I can't drink another drop,' her visitor answers. Fired up with a sudden burst of energy, she stands up and shakes out her skirt. 'Time I was off. May I meet the children before I leave?'

Margaret nods. It is a pity Lavinia is getting ready to leave. After so long, it is delightful to talk to another woman. Margaret bites her lip.

'Can I tell you a secret? I haven't even told Wallace yet.'

'Oh yes, please. I do love secrets. They're so scarce in Shillong. The gossips here make sure everybody knows everything.'

Margaret blushes and places a hand on her belly. 'I'm expecting a baby.'

'Oh, dear heart, do I congratulate you, or do I commiserate?'

Wallace is glad to be leaving Shillong; to travel across country and visit places he had never seen. He has had enough of the company of his wife and family, the evenings at the golf club that Margaret revels in. Only four weeks or so, he reassures her. He will be home well before her confinement. The company has asked him to look into the possibility of a new tea plantation farther into Meghalaya, in a place a good four days ride from Shillong and then, on to a potato farm that is suffering a bout of blight. He suspects his departure suits Margaret. She is in her sixth month and, as she says herself, is waddling like a goose. The ayah Baia keeps the three little girls under her care as neat as new pins and is clever enough to be deaf to Margaret's temper. Meanwhile he is free to travel into new territory, the rain seeping through his clothes as he watches out for snakes, for the thunder of elephants, the pad of a tiger deep among the trees. Farming back home in Ireland is dull and tedious in comparison. This is husbandry of a wildly different sort: a fight against the wantonness of vine, bark and leaf. Such an exotic, fecund land stirs in him a desire to subjugate it.

Dawn is breaking when Wallace sets out with his Khasi guide Bon who is bald as an egg and as strong as a horse. Bon travels with him everywhere. Baia is the only other person awake in the house. On the veranda the ayah stands, a short, round figure in her robe and with tiny bare feet, watching while they pack up the ponies. When they are ready to leave, she darts down the steps to fill their pockets with freshly-made *jadoh* wrapped in leaves and then she hands a bottle of *kyat* to Bon. Wallace checks the ponies' girths. Bon makes a step of his intertwined fingers for Wallace to scramble onto the pony. He settles into his saddle so clumsily that the ayah throws up her hands to cover her face and hide her laughter.

Wallace decides to surprise her.

'*Khublei*, Baia.'

On hearing the Khasi salutation, her face lights up.

They have not travelled far along the forest trail when Wallace pulls on his reins.

'What is in the bottle?'

Bon shrugs. 'For the thirst, babu.'

There is a touch of military precision about the Khasi. Bon learnt English when working for the 44th Gurkha battalion before they left Shillong. He sits upright on his saddle, on his guard.

'Give it to me.'

With reluctance, the guide hands him the bottle. Wallace uncorks it and lets the liquid flow out onto the grass. 'We're not taking firewater with us.'

Bon's eyes widen. His expression is impassive.

As the weeks pass, Margaret spends her time at Ward's Lake with the girls and Baia. The man-made lake, fringed with vegetation, is a popular place in Shillong for families from the European quarter. The lake is in the shape of a horseshoe. A lucky sign, Margaret thinks, although she doesn't believe in luck. Spanning the lake is a wooden bridge leading to gaily painted tea rooms. Grassy lawns slope to the water's edge. Geese and ducks splash in the water. There are punts for hire tied up on the banks. Ward's Lake reminds Margaret of the pond in St Stephen's Green. All those unseen hands trimming the hedges, painting the railings, keeping everything tidy.

While Wallace is away, her days are her own. Today the children play on the banks of the lake. Maggie has a little sailing boat on a string and Elizabeth, thumb in her mouth, kneels to watch the boat bob in the water. Suddenly she makes a grab for the string.

'It's my go!'

'No, it's not,' the older child grips the string. 'I said *no.*'

'You're a meanie,' Elizabeth wails. When she flings herself at her mother, 'stop that silliness at once!' Margaret snaps, her voice loud enough to carry across the lake. The little girls scowl at each other. The ayah spreads out a rug on the grass and sets out the contents of the picnic basket. The children abandon the boat and settle down to eat their sandwiches in silence. Margaret closes her eyes and lies back in the chair. She feels listless, empty. Around her, other families are seated on the lawns. Why can't you two go and play with those children? she is about to say when her attention is caught.

'Such a peaceful picture you make, Mrs McKay!'

She struggles to her feet, mountainous in her loose gown. Gazing at her with pity in their eyes are the Reverend George Peacock and his wife.

'Not long to go now, I see,' Mildred Peacock says. She taps the ground with her umbrella and wonders if it might rain. She has a high voice, a spindly neck and greying hair pulled into a bun. Her husband is a man in his fifties, his eyes watering behind thick-lensed spectacles. They are so alike, they remind Margaret of a pair of scrawny chickens trussed up together for market. Such tiresome people, she thinks. The Peacocks are Methodist missionaries, committed to bringing Christianity to the Orient. They worked in China until Mr Peacock fell ill. 'We have come to Shillong to recuperate,' Mildred once explained to Margaret, 'while we continue God's work among the Khasi people. He has chosen not to bless us with children in order that we can work tirelessly on His behalf.'

Those Holy Joes, Margaret said to Wallace privately after meeting them for the first time, they had better not try and convert *me*.

'How is Mr McKay?'

'Oh, he'll be back in the next few days,' Margaret says. 'He is up country at present but I'm expecting him home by the end of the week.'

Again, the pitying look in the woman's face. 'It's hard to be so far from home at a time like this. If you need anything, please just ask me.'

'Oh, I have Mrs Brewster coming to deliver me, which is a great relief,' Margaret says. 'I am very grateful to her. It's a long way for her to travel but I couldn't manage without her.'

In silence they watch as three young women, twirling their parasols, cross the bridge. Such a pretty sight they make, Margaret sighs, if only she could enjoy it alone. Above the lake dark clouds are gathering.

'May I be so forward as to ask you a question, Mrs McKay?'

It is the husband now, peering at her under his straw hat. She is reminded of a marmoset: those thick goggle-like lenses, the little nose quivering.

Margaret makes an effort to be gracious. 'Of course.'

A digit finger touching his lips, his breast bone. Delicately he clears his throat. Heavens, she wonders, is he about to sing? Mr Peacock turns to look at the girls playing with the boat in the water before speaking.

'Have you brought your little ones to be baptised yet?'

She is scalded by the man's effrontery. What gives these people licence? Their claim to a superior knowledge makes them crusaders against the heathen, and now they are marshalling against her. Mr Peacock is no better than she is and yet he feels he has a God-given right to interrogate her. For a moment Margaret is speechless. In her home, in her head and her heart, the relationship she has with the Lord is her concern alone. It does not belong in Mr Peacock's world of piety.

'My children do not need to be baptised.'

He presses home his message: anything can befall an innocent child here: fever, snake bites, a sudden native outbreak, a wild tiger. 'Even in Shillong, we are never fully safe from disaster, my dear. The gates of Heaven are close by for all of us, even the littlest among us but only if we obey God's law. In a state of grace, a child is welcome in His congregation, isn't that a wonderful gift?' Surely she would wish that her children be armed to withstand the worst depredations of this heathen place?

She speaks as if she hasn't heard a word, the low tone of her voice matching his. 'My husband and I don't belong to your congregation. We do not believe that infants should be enlisted at baptism like raw recruits.'

'Without God,' he intones, 'there is no hope.'

Has the man not heard what she has said?

'For your information, Mr Peacock, we are Unitarians.'

She is aware of a silent, bowed presence: the ayah is standing too close to her for comfort. Margaret is suffused with a sudden rage. What is Baia thinking of, a woman who is just a servant? Her throat tightens. On every side, tormentors are out to destroy her peace of mind.

'Go away!' she shouts at the ayah, raising a hand to strike her. Baia slips away out of her reach and pads down to join the children at the water's edge. At the sight of the angry, heavily-pregnant woman who looks as if she is about to hit him too, Mr Peacock steps back.

Margaret glares at him. 'We do not subscribe to any creed, we depend on ourselves, on our intelligence, as well as on the guidance of reason and conscience to teach us how to live, *Mr* Peacock.'

The missionary moves further out of her range, fixing his cuffs nervously as he goes, saying, 'We must be going, my dear.'

His wife emits a high-pitched giggle and takes his arm with alacrity. He lifts his hat. For a moment his eyes as pale as boiled sweets rest on Margaret.

'Please extend our good wishes to Mr McKay,' he says before tramping away across the lawn, his wife on his arm, his words, *sotto voce* trailing after him, 'May the Lord be good to the unfortunate man.'

When Wallace returns, ruddy faced and lean, he fills the bungalow with his presence: his coat smells of chillies and cumin, his feet are blistered. In his pockets are toys for the girls and a bundle of letters for Margaret which he has collected at the station. On his first night he sleeps for fifteen hours, dreaming through the relentless monsoon rains. Rain swirls and eddies around the veranda, trickles down the chimneys, beats on the windowpanes. The fires are kept lit all day and a somnolence takes hold. They are like two beached whales: Wallace stretched out in a basket chair on one side of the fire, Margaret sitting on the other side. He talks about his travels, the great waterfalls, the river bridges made from woven roots of trees, spanning deep gorges.

'Margaret,' he says, his voice shy with excitement, 'the fertility of the land, you would not believe.'

Occasionally they play canasta. It reminds her of their journey from England on board ship: the cabin-like room, the way they made do with each other's company. Wallace laughs when Margaret tells him about her encounter with the Methodists. His voice is startlingly loud. Each time he returns from his travels, she must adapt to having a man in the house again and the disruption makes her feel cross.

'I don't understand why people have to meddle,' she grumbles.

'They are competing for our souls, I suppose. Shillong is stuffed with missionaries. They must like it here.'

'And not a Unitarian to be found,' she sighs. 'It would make a pleasant change to be with one's own.'

'*I* am with you now.'

'Aye, and next week you'll be gone again.'

'Only be for a few days, I promise. Mrs Brewster will be here soon when the little man is ready to arrive.'

They have got into the habit of referring to the expected baby as if they know it is a boy. *Little man. Baby Wallace.* It is tempting fate, she thinks, but there is no harm in it. After three girls it's only fair to expect that the baby will be a boy.

Anyway, this pregnancy feels different, she convinces herself, the baby kicking like a donkey and giving her dyspepsia.

Only for a few days, Wallace promised, a week at most, but the week turns into ten days. The waiting drags out her bad humour, exacerbates the pains in her legs and back.

When at last she hears the ponies at the gate she hurries out onto the veranda and, to her astonishment, finds that her husband is not alone. A European woman is sitting on the pack horse. She is in her early twenties, stockily built, wears her hair short and is dressed like a Khasi woman, in a *ka jympien*, the checked cotton cloth knotted over one shoulder.

'I found the Reverend Barr lost in the forest,' Wallace says, with a wave of his hand as introduction. 'She had a native guide with her but he was worse than useless. It was fortunate I came across the two of them.'

The Reverend Barr?

Margaret stares at the young woman who, having dismounted from her horse, is coming up the veranda steps towards her, smiling.

'I think I'd have managed quite well, but it was kind of your husband to come to my aid,' the woman says. 'I do hope, Mr McKay, that you will call in to my village the next time you are passing. That way I can repay your kindness.'

Then she turns to Margaret and thrusts out her hand. 'Mrs McKay, it is a great pleasure to meet you.'

'Where on earth have you come from?'

'Eee, mam, all tha way from Rotherham,' Miss Barr says in an exaggerated north of England accent.

'Oh, pardon me, I didn't mean ...'

Wallace rocks back on his heels, enjoying his wife's discomfort. 'You asked for the company of one of our own.

My dear, you'll be glad to know that the Reverend Barr is a Unitarian missionary.'

'No, Mr McKay,' the visitor is quick to contradict him. 'I am not a missionary. I am a teacher. My desire is to live up to Gandhiji's instruction.'

'Gandhiji?' Margaret says faintly.

'You've surely heard of him: the great leader, Mr Gandhi. I was privileged to meet him in Wardha. My sister is working there on his behalf. I asked him for guidance and do you know what he said?'

'I have no idea.'

'Gandhiji told me to give up being a missionary and to find some constructive work in the villages. He posed a question that I couldn't answer: what else is worth doing in comparison to serving those who need you most? That's the reason I'm here in Meghalaya: to set up a school for the tribal children. They are so poor, they have nothing.'

The young woman yawns noisily and continues. 'He gave me the best advice.'

Now Wallace is curious. 'What kind of advice?'

She ignores him, smiles at Margaret. 'Gandhiji advised me not to get mixed up in politics and to stay out of jail.'

Margaret cannot take her eyes off her. She is entranced by Miss Barr's self-assurance, the simplicity of her clothes, her big, rough hands energetically swatting away the flies that are buzzing around her head.

'Please come inside. You must have some tea.'

'Right now, I need more than tea,' Miss Barr says. 'I could eat a horse.'

The pudding is being served up when Margaret shakes the brass hand bell at her elbow. The door opens and the ayah leads the three little girls in to meet the visitor and to say goodnight to their parents. Dutifully Miss Barr *ooohs* and *aaahs* over the children. Then, to Margaret's surprise, the visitor puts her hand on Baia's arm and asks after her mother. Bobbing with pleasure, the ayah answers before she leads away the children.

Margaret is mystified. 'How do you know Baia?'

'Oh, I've known Baia since I came to Meghalaya. She and her family are members of our congregation.'

It takes a moment for Margaret to absorb the news. The ayah is a free thinker. *What will I discover next: that the gardener is a university professor?*

'I had no idea.'

'All the time she has lived under our roof,' Wallace guffaws, 'and we never thought.'

'Well, it's good to know,' Margaret says. 'At least, Baia won't be filling the girls' heads with silly heathen notions.'

It is a pity, Miss Barr thinks, that Mrs McKay doesn't laugh more often. She has a sunny countenance with her rosy complexion and intelligent eyes. Even in her late pregnancy, she is a handsome woman. But Margaret is unaware of Miss Barr's unspoken admiration. She is lost in thought: *that day at Ward's Lake, Baia came and stood beside her when Mr Peacock was being so rude. Could it be that the ayah, in her own way, was trying to lend her support?* She shakes her head. *How annoying to have a servant who is forward in her ways.*

'I suppose, Miss Barr, you are responsible for converting Baia?' Wallace says.

'No, not at all. Our Khasi movement is unique: you could say that it has sprung from the soil of Meghalaya. We didn't come and convert them. They came to us. We have their founder to thank: an extraordinary man, Mr Kissor Singh.'

Wallace shrugs, 'I've never heard of him.'

'Well, you are in danger of hearing everything I know about him. Mr Singh is a hero of mine. He is a Khasi who was converted by the Welsh missionaries at an early age.'

Margaret groans. 'Oh, those Methodists.'

'Yes, indeed.'

Wallace raises an eyebrow.

Miss Barr continues, 'Mr Singh concluded that the Welsh Reform faith was simply replacing the Khasi fear of demons with the fear of hell. Much to the Methodists' annoyance, he left and went on to spread his message among his own people. He spoke to them about the unity of God, the Brotherhood of man, about love, union, worship, and the absence of fear. And these, as you know, are all the tenets we hold dear.'

'How remarkable,' Wallace says.

The visitor dabs her mouth with her napkin. 'You see, Mr Kissor Singh became a Unitarian, without knowing that anyone else in the world thought like he did. Eventually, he made contact with an American Unitarian in Calcutta, a gentleman called Mr Dall, I believe, and discovered that he wasn't alone. Today there are three Unitarian churches in Meghalaya, thanks to Mr Singh. The members believe in one God, they help one another when in difficulty and sing their hymns on Sundays just as lustily as we do.' Miss Barr pauses. 'But I must stress the Khasi people came to us by their own route.'

Margaret can tell Wallace has lost interest in the conversation while she is intrigued by the visitor. If I hadn't married, she wonders, and was free to go my own way, would I have her courage? Just then the young woman rests her hand on Margaret's sleeve. 'Mrs McKay, that meal was such a treat after the native food I've grown accustomed to eating.'

Margaret reddens with pleasure. 'Oh, Miss Barr thank you. Please go on.'

'What more can I tell you? You probably know about the place held by women in Khasi culture.'

At this point Wallace pushes back his chair and stands up. 'I must leave you, ladies. Agricultural reports don't write themselves.'

As the door closes behind him, Miss Barr bites her lip. 'I'm sorry if I was boring him. He's been so kind.'

'Ach, Lord, don't mind Wallace. He's been travelling in the forest for too long and has forgotten his manners. I would love to hear more.'

Miss Barr looked thoughtful. 'The position of Khasi women is unique in the world.'

'You surprise me. I find them slow to adapt to our ways.'

'Well, do you know of any other society where the women are more than equal than the men? For instance, here in Meghalaya, inheritance comes to the youngest daughter and not to the eldest son, as in the Western world.'

'What a splendid idea!' Margaret's enthusiasm is genuine. 'The youngest daughter gets the property and she is best suited to take care of elderly parents. Why, she can be the safety net for the whole family.'

Miss Barr munches a piece of bread as she talks. 'In other parts of India, marriages are arranged by the parents. Here it is left to the young people to make their own choice. After they marry, the groom usually goes to live in the house of the bride's mother, not the other way round.'

Margaret sits back, her hands on her swollen belly. 'I didn't know this.'

'They are an eminently practical people and their customs arise from the simple nature of Khasi society.'

Margaret breathes. 'Simplicity is the key to a good life.'

'I agree. It's also considered unwise to marry a widow. Apparently a Khasi widow walks in the next world with her first husband, and a succeeding husband must walk at her heels like a dog.'

The sound of their laughter, rich and unexpected, bounces around the room.

'Oh, my goodness!' Margaret gasps. 'Our suffragettes could learn a thing or two.'

Miss Barr looks solemn and folds her hands, as if in prayer. 'In their statement of faith, the Khasi declare their belief in the Fatherhood of God, just like we do, but, unlike us, they declare an equal belief in the Motherhood of God.'

Until that day, the only women Margaret has known in India are Lavinia Frobisher and the wives at the golf club, who talk incessantly about their children and servants. Now this stranger from Rotherham has reached into her soul.

She leans forward and whispers, 'The *Motherhood* of God?'

'Yes,' Miss Barr dimples, 'I know.'

With a sigh, Margaret announces to the dining table that is waiting to be cleared, 'Well, I can truly say that is the most remarkable article of religious faith I have ever heard.'

As the two women sit in companionable silence, their thoughts range beyond the boundaries of their lives. *What might be* ... is a shared, tantalizing gleam in the darkening room.

VIII

'How many days to your birthday?'

Uncertainly, the little girl displays her fingers.

'Take away one,' Margaret says, pressing down a little finger. 'It is in nine days' time.'

'Will there be a cake?'

'There will be a cake and your friends will be here for the party.'

Maggie squeezes her eyes with delight. 'Oh, Mummy!'

How easy it is to make a child happy, Margaret thinks, her cheek resting on her daughter's head. Even if she teaches Maggie everything she knows, the girl is growing fast and has so much more to learn.

'And how many candles will there be on the cake?' she asks, but Maggie has spied a butterfly quivering on the floor. She slides out of her mother's arms. A flash of electric blue rises through the open door, and flutters onto the veranda with Maggie chasing after it.

Margaret is relieved when Mrs Brewster arrives, fatter than ever, red-faced and sodden in a mountainous gaberdine coat. After examining Margaret, she frowns.

'It's not good,' she says.

'What do you mean?'

'At a guess, I'd say you are two weeks' overdue.' Mrs Brewster removes a bottle from her satchel and carefully pours a spoonful of pale liquid. Margaret closes her eyes. When the liquid hits the back of her throat she splutters and yellow droplets spray onto her blouse.

'You've spilt half of it down your front. I'll double the dose tomorrow.'

From then on, Mrs Brewster ignores her. She settles down to dinner over a half bottle of whiskey while she and Wallace exchange opinions on the best method for breaking horses. That night, Margaret retires early. She sleeps soundly until, at dawn, she wakes to find that her labour has started. The castor oil has worked. In the grey dawn she is gripped by a sudden terror.

'Dear Lord, help me through this trial,' she prays. 'And, please, please let it be a boy.'

At the beginning she is able to walk about the bedroom but as the hours elongate into evening, her labour pains strengthen and she has to lie down. The muscular spasms chase one another, faster and faster, until everything is lost in a blur. She is desperate to force a way out of her pain, but Mrs Brewster, crouched at the end of the bed, now comes up close, the smell of whiskey still on her breath.

'No, Mrs McKay, you are *not* to push.'

Margaret moans. 'I can't help myself.'

Mrs Brewster is adamant.

Outside it is night and, through the open window, a star peeps under the eaves. The world is at peace while she is conscious of a foul, faecal smell. Her bowels are out of control, her body shaking and slimy with sweat: she has become an animal clawing at the sheets.

'What time is it?' she wants to know. Her voice is pitiful. In the lull before the next contraction, she vows that she will *never, ever* suffer this indignity again. Mrs Brewster does not hear. Margaret closes her eyes. If it is a boy, a girl or puppy dog, she couldn't care less.

'What time is it?' she asks again through cracked lips. There is no answer. No comfort to be had: nothing to hold back the tidal wave. With a scream, she feels herself go under.

Just then, Mrs Brewster stands up. Rolled-up sleeves on fleshy arms, her bright moon face glistening, her mouth, contorted in triumph.

'Push, Margaret, push for all you're worth ...'

Sitting at his desk, Wallace is trying to concentrate. Whenever he opens a book, the words swim before his eyes, so he gives up and reaches instead for the newspaper his mother sent him in the post. *The Freeman's Journal* is five weeks old but news from home is always welcome. The markets section in the paper catches his attention. There has been 'considerable friction and unpleasantness upon the reopening of the London tea sales.' Those traders should be forced to spend time out here in Assam, he thinks, they might appreciate the sweat and toil. Without the planters they would have no tea to bicker over.

The traders aren't the only ones out of touch. He is cocooned in this godforsaken part of India. He tries to follow the reports. A mammoth air raid on London. German aerodrome bombed in Belgium. Chinese Civil War. The whole world is tearing itself apart. And somewhere inside that world is his brother. Alive or dead. The General List of War Casualties fills an entire column of the newspaper. James McKay is not listed. Wallace's thoughts lead back to

Seacon, to his family living in an island of sanity, while around them the province is drowning in intransigence. It irks him to think of Orangemen and politicians cleaving to the yoke of the British Empire. Not that the other side is any better: de Valera and his mob of dangerous idealists. Fanatics. It is a simple matter: Home Rule is inevitable, no matter how much Mr Carson and his ilk squawk about it. The war will end in victory, and Home Rule will be established. Surely to heaven, Wallace thinks, common sense will prevail.

He becomes aware of a presence at the door. For a split second, he thinks that his mother is standing there, with news of James. Then he sees Baia, the ayah, in her white robe. Her face is aglow and she is clamouring for attention. Wallace hears her voice but her words don't register.

What?

As she bends near him, the ayah is awed by the sight of his fingers, splayed on the newspaper. Alongside her little brown hands resting on the polished wooden desk, his fingers look gigantic.

'Babu,' she says, 'I'm telling you the truth. It is a boy.'

Then he understands. Wallace gives a howl of joy and hides his face in his hands.

A stick of incense burns low in the bedroom. Margaret looks ethereally beautiful, her hair spread out on the pillow, in a fresh nightgown, any evidence of her ordeal wrapped up and secreted away.

'Well now, Wallace, you have what you wanted.'

For a moment he doesn't reply. In his study, in front of Baia, he broke down and wept. Now he is empty of feeling. 'Yes, indeed I have.'

Margaret is disappointed. After what she has endured, this is all he can say. She holds up the infant. 'Say hello to your son.'

'Will you look at the little man?' Wallace leans over, his lips brushing the infant's head. 'He is as yellow as a Chinaman.'

Her grip tightens. No, she thinks, he is my beauty.

'Just a touch of jaundice,' Mrs Brewster says from her vantage point at the window. 'I've seen it in newborns. Disappears in a day or two. You just keep feeding him, Mrs McKay.'

'Yes,' Margaret lies back on the pillows. She is so tired she would agree to anything.

'Oh, my dearest,' Wallace wants to tell her how grateful he is, how humbled. She has borne him a son: it is a miracle. He grasps her hand and squeezes it. He is conscious that the midwife is watching his every move. If they were alone, he would wrap his wife in his arms and rock her.

'Darling wife,' he whispers in her ear, 'I am so proud of you.'

But Margaret has drifted away to sleep.

The following day Mrs Brewster starts her journey back to Tezpur. Wallace goes to the gate to see her off. A servant leads down her pony, saddled up and whinnying to be off.

'Thank you, Mrs Brewster,' Wallace says, 'for the care you have given my wife.'

'And the dear infant,' she prompts.

'Of course,' he smiles, 'and baby Wallace.'

They shake hands formally.

As she reaches for the pony's bridle, she says archly, 'Now you'll be able to shave off that moustache of yours.'

He is mystified. 'I beg your pardon?'

The crouching servant offers his clasped hands to form a step for Mrs Brewster. The midwife pulls herself up and sits astride the horse. Gripping the reins, she looks at Wallace. To his astonishment, she winks.

'You're a man now,' she says. 'You have a son, so that awful moustache can go.'

Margaret is furious when Wallace tells her what the midwife said.

'I can't believe she said that. The cheek of her.'

He regrets he told her: it takes so little to get Margaret into a lather.

'Darling, take it easy. The baby –'

'There's nothing wrong with the baby.'

'You need to rest.' He worries over her, tucks in the sheets and plumps the pillows.

'Ach, will ye stop your fussing.'

'I wish you'd do what you're told, Mrs McKay.'

She softens. 'Oh, you have no idea how relieved I am to see the back of that woman.'

'You mean Mrs Bossy Boots?'

She yelps with delight. Her cool fingers touch his cheek.

'A boy,' he murmurs, bending over the cradle. 'I still can't believe it.'

Margaret is exultant. She has done it: she has made her husband a slave to happiness.

Wallace straightens up, lanky and awkward. 'You'll have to depend on me to run the household until you're up and about.'

'Baia will keep the cook in line.'

'The children have promised to be good. Are you well enough for a visit from them? They're as keen as mustard to see the wee lad.'

Wallace, the least vain of men, is preening like a peacock. She wonders aloud if it is sinful to be so proud? And he laughs and says, 'Maybe a little, but I think God will forgive us both.'

Contentedly, she snuggles down in the bed, listening to noises beyond the bedroom door: the scurrying here and there, the banging doors, her daughters' voices. She is the heart of the household. Four beautiful children, and one of them a little prince: it is too much joy for any woman to bear. She peers over the side of the bed at the infant in his cot. Mrs Brewster is right: his yellowness is fading already.

Mrs Brewster said the baby would be fine and dandy and Margaret believes her. There is no reason to worry, although he has not taken to the breast the way his sisters have. He does not cry but lies still, his little chest rising and falling. To his sister Elizabeth, the baby looks like a doll. Standing on her tiptoes to peer into the cot she asks, 'What's his name, Mammy?'

'He will be called Wallace, like your father.'

Her sister touches the baby's cheek and instantly recoils. 'Why is he so hot?'

'Mrs Brewster says he'll be fine and dandy.'

For a moment Margaret wonders if the baby is alright. He seems feverish, his little face screwed up and whimpering.

'It's nothing,' she says, 'just the jaundice.'

'Mammy will come to my birthday party,' Maggie tells her younger sister, 'and baby Wallace too. Isn't that right, Mammy?'

'My darling, we wouldn't miss it for the world.'

Throughout the night, the baby is restless, making sharp, anxious sounds. Margaret holds him close, but he fights her with a scowling mouth and eyes tight shut. Try to suck, my dearest one, she whispers, pressing his mouth to her breast. It is of no use: the baby arches his back and screams. Whenever Margaret tries to feed him, he resists. Her breasts engorged, the milk soaking her nightdress. Fear in her throat. Suck, little man, suck, she begs, but he won't. Or can't. His skin is burning, his breath comes in short, fat bursts. Early in the morning, his cries trail away and the bedroom is quiet. She lies back, exhausted, the infant in her arms, and sleeps.

When she opens her eyes, terror stabs her. *Where is the baby? Has he died in the night?* But he is lying beside her, fast asleep. It has been a bad dream, all is well, but when she lifts him up, his body is on fire. Once more she offers him her breast and again his mouth slips off the nipple. She is frightened by the tiny gasping sounds he makes. She is so far from home, from her sister Molly who knows everything about babies. Even her mother, old as she is, would know what to do. Margaret fights off a gust of panic. She must stay strong. She must help him to pull through. Over the years she has guided other people's children, foreign children, in her care. She remembers each one: Jacob Cohen, Sarah Oldman. And there were the others: Esther Silverstone, Bessie Jacobson, all of them gone out into the world now, able to read and write, thanks to her, and to do their multiplication tables. In her own way, she saved those children who were cast adrift from their homeland and were desperate to learn. She lifts the baby's head to her breast. He lets out a piercing cry. She will be strong for him. *Baruch Haba* ... yes, that was Sarah Oldman's favourite saying, she remembers: Blessed is the one who comes.

The next day Dr Mackintosh arrives from the old army hospital, wheezing, his waistcoat stained with tobacco juice, his basset hound eyes brimming with unshed tears. He barely looks at the baby, tells Margaret to keep feeding him and then walks out of the bedroom before she has a chance to question him.

In the hallway her husband and the doctor speak in low mumbles. When Wallace comes into the bedroom, Margaret is frantic.

'What did he say?'

Wallace's face is grey, his hair tousled. He has slept fitfully on the sofa in the drawing room to be close by, in case Margaret needed him.

For a moment, as if absent-mindedly, he rubs his face. Then he looks at her, a sudden anguish in his eyes. 'Margaret.'

'What?'

'Dr Mackintosh said we should pray.'

'No!'

Hair flying, fists clenched, Margaret rises up in the bed, spittle on her cheek. Her rage is so explosive that the windowpanes shiver. Startled by the noise, the baby in her arms whimpers.

'Get you on out of here and shut the door behind you,' she screams, 'and take that mouldy old quack with you.'

'Margaret, dearest ...' Wallace lays his hand on her arm, but she'll have none of it.

From then on, the ayah is the only person allowed to enter the bedroom. At mealtimes Baia brings in a tray of food. An hour later, she comes out with the food hardly touched. Wallace is reduced to prowling like a caged animal around the bungalow. To be shut out is unbearable and yet, in a way, it is a relief. He is worse than useless: a big lummock of a man who knows all there is to know about the science of tea, and nothing at all about birth. Or death. As the hours pass, his agitation changes to a whining emptiness. He tries to pray but no words come. He sits, the

Bible open before him. His only thought: if God chooses to take the baby, no prayer of mine will stop Him. Whenever the ayah comes, face to face, with Wallace loitering outside the bedroom door or sitting in the drawing room, staring into space, she gives an imperceptible shake of her head.

'Any word?'

'No, babu.'

'Tell Mr McKay,' Margaret's tone is crisp, 'that Maggie's birthday party must be cancelled. The baby needs peace and quiet.'

An ignorant girl like that, how can she possibly understand? Then she sees the ayah's frightened eye. *She knows.*

When she hears about the birthday party, little Maggie lets out a wail and throws herself, sobbing, on the sofa. Frightened by her distress, her two sisters join in, crying piteously. It is the last straw. Wallace bundles the children into the care of Mrs Frobisher who, to his surprise, responds with alacrity when he asks her. In times like these, he says, you certainly know who your friends are.

Without the children, the bungalow hollows into a heartsick chamber. The bedroom door stays closed. A mother knows best, Wallace tells himself. He must be patient, although he knows, deep in his heart, it is hopeless. He has never felt so alone. His natural reserve cannot protect him. He misses Margaret, misses her conversation; her dry wit. More often than not, when they are seated at dinner, he finds himself half-listening to her: there is only so much domestic trivia a man could take. Now the shadows in the dining room are malevolent, pressing in on him. The meat congeals on his plate, the pudding goes cold. Eventually he cannot bear the loneliness any longer. Carrying one of the chairs from the dining room, he positions it outside the bedroom door and sits down.

Leaning his face against the panelled teak, he hears the faint cry of the baby's distress. He murmurs, 'My dearest, I am here.'

There was no response on that day, nor on the day after.

On the fourth day Wallace wakes to an apparition: a figure standing in the open door of the bedroom with a bundle in her arms. A grotesque version of Margaret: her nightgown, soiled and creased, her feet bare, her face ghastly with grief. The glory of her nut-brown hair that he loved from the moment he saw her for the first time in St Stephen's Green church is no more. Suffering has turned her hair snow white.

'Oh Wallace,' she sobs. 'I couldn't pray.'

'It will be alright,' he says, opening his arms to her but when she comes into his embrace, the little corpse, cold against his chest, is a knife in his heart.

IX

The Reverend Barr comes to pray with them. She stays the night and on the following day, the baby is buried in the old army cemetery.

'My baby in the cold ground,' Margaret moans, 'I cannot bear to think of it.'

'Be strong, dear Mrs McKay,' Miss Barr says. 'Your baby is happy now. Somewhere on High, God is smiling upon him.'

Four weeks after the burial, Wallace sets out on a lengthy tour of the tea gardens at Nazirah, Deopani, Mazengah and Mackeypore. In a sombre mood he leaves behind a grieving household. It doesn't take long for his spirits to rise: his boyish taste for adventure is as keen as ever. The guide, Bon, accompanies him as they ride on horseback for the first four days. When the forest becomes too difficult for the horses, they travel by elephant. I must make a ridiculous sight, Wallace thinks, an ungainly figure in a rough construction of wooden rails strapped on the elephant's back. His long legs are cramped and sore. Thankfully there is no one to see him except Bon who sits cross-legged behind him and the mahout urging on the elephant whenever it stops to eat from the trees. At last, the forest falls away and they are blinded by sunlight. Shading his eyes, Wallace takes out his compass.

'Not much farther to go.'

As the elephant ambles through the brilliance of noon, Wallace slips in and out of sleep, dreaming of Seacon on a windy day, sheets flying on the clothesline. Then, startled by the mahout's shout, he struggles awake, his skin prickling with fear.

There is nothing more than a ripple of movement through the grass. Wallace can't figure out what it is but when the tiger breaks cover, he freezes. It is huge, golden, black-striped, terrifying. The tiger springs and the startled elephant rears back, while the mahout desperately holds on. Wallace recalls his father clinging to the old roof while he mended a hole in the thatch, an incongruous thought at a time like this. The tiger sinks back into the grass. Nothing moves. Only for a moment. Snarling, the animal rises again, in a frenzy. Higher, this time, and so near, its bared teeth close on the mahout's bamboo whip. The man screams. Wallace can't move: his legs are too stiff. He is helpless while, beneath him, the elephant sways in an exaggerated waltz of panic.

Wallace senses, rather than sees, Bon straighten up, lift his rifle and fire. The shot cracks open the grassy plain, sending small creatures scurrying. The bellying sound of gunfire is followed by a profound silence. Shaking, Wallace bends over the rail of the howdah and vomits. He sits back, appalled by his own weakness, and wipes his mouth with his handkerchief. As the elephant begins its slow progress, he slumps back, mortified. Bon takes charge, leaning forward and shouting at the mahout to stop. Wallace rouses himself, turns towards the man who has saved his life and says, 'What a magnificent shot! I promise you will have your fill of *kyat* when we get to Nazirah.'

Bon's face breaks out in a grin. 'First you have some *chai*.'

Tea: a tonic, hot and fresh. It is just what Wallace needs. He hunkers down with Bon beside the fire, grateful when the guide hands him the steaming tin mug. His spirits lift. It is enough, he thinks, simply to be alive.

The mahout looks up from his task of skinning the tiger and shouts.

'What did he say?'

'He says it is a mamma tiger,' Bon says, 'so baby tigers near. He wants to know if you shoot them.'

Wallace closes his eyes. He can feel the chill of a little body against his heart.

His throat tightens. 'No.'

Bon shrugs. The two men drink their chai in silence while the mahout continues skinning the carcass, his knife flicking in the sunlight. Buzzards circle high in the sky. In this country, death is never far away, Wallace thinks and, inexplicably, the thought gives him comfort.

He arrives back to Shillong to find that Margaret is no longer in her mourning clothes. The mood in the bungalow has lifted. The little girls come tumbling and laughing towards him. His wife is wearing a soft blue dress with lacy cuffs and collar, her white hair pulled back into a bun.

She looks grave. 'There's a letter for you in the study.'

In the pile of correspondence on his desk, the small grey envelope stands out. The penny stamp with the head of King Edward VII. The thick black border. His mother writing with news that his father has died. As he reads the letter Wallace feels guilty at how relieved he is. Thanks be to the Lord. James, his brother is safe.

The shock was great and we are very desolate and lonely but at the bottom of my heart I know how much we have to be thankful for. Your father had no extra suffering and he had got so infirm that it was only his strong will that kept him about. You are sure to feel very sad about your father and for your comfort I must tell you how very much he valued your letters and how when the war caused them to be irregular in coming if he was ever disappointed not getting one, he took an old letter and read it. He was sorry about the little son and that you took it so hardly, his memory was greatly gone but he still remembered his own family, it was like this, he would ask one thing over and over. Your sisters join with me in love to you and yours. Your loving Mother, E. McKay.

He is moved at the thought that, brainsick as his father was, he felt pity on the loss of his grandson. Or maybe, his mother has put words in a dead man's mouth. *As placid as a sleeping child* ... there are worse ways to go. He gives the letter to Margaret.

'I am sorry for your trouble, Wallace,' but she is unmoved. Wallace's father kept himself at a distance whenever they visited Seacon. She doubts if he even knew the names of his grandchildren.

'Eighty-six years of age!' Wallace says, 'he had a good life.'

His head sinks into his chest. A vase of roses in the window emits a funereal sweetness.

'Dinner will be served soon.'

He rouses himself. 'Tell me what you've been doing.'

She has been playing bridge at the club three days a week. Lavinia Frobisher is her partner and they have such fun.

'And how are the children?'

Her expression becomes anxious. 'I worry about them all the time. Wallace, you must make the decision. The time is coming to send the children home. Maggie and Elizabeth are ready for school.'

'What about Alexandra?'

'She is too little for school but can be put with my sister, Molly. It's not safe here in India.'

'It's better that Alexandra stay with my mother and the girls,' he says. 'They've suffered such a loss, it will do them good. I'll write to Mam right away. She will be wondering why a letter hasn't come.'

As far as Margaret is concerned, Alexandra can be placed wherever Wallace wishes. To be going home is all that matters to her. She aches to see her two sisters again, and her friend, Alice. Even her father, bedridden since he had fallen off his bicycle. *The foolish man*, her sister wrote, *cycling around the county for his beloved Liberal party. Fat lot of good it did him. He is nothing more than a cripple now and a bad-tempered one at that. Our poor sister, Jane is run ragged minding him ...*

It will be a strange homecoming, Margaret thinks.

After dinner they sit in the drawing room in silence. For Wallace, it is a comfort to be home and find everything the way it was. More or less. Under his feet, the new tiger skin is resplendent before the fire grate and, in the soldiers' cemetery, the grass has grown over his son's resting place. Time moves on, he thinks, and we are powerless to do anything about it.

He gazes at his wife. 'What about the journey? Will you feel strong enough to travel when the time comes?'

'Ach, I'm as right as rain. The trip will do me good.'

'As soon as this war is over, then you should go.'

She sighs. 'Will it ever end?'

'We must pray to God that James stays safe until it does.'

That night he falls into a dreamless sleep. When he wakes, an early mist outside has made a white sanctuary of their bedroom. He stretches out on his back and thinks again about his lucky escape. It's a story good enough for the men at the club. Beside him, Margaret's sleeping body is warm, the sheet thrown back to reveal her rucked up nightgown, a crescent of white flesh. He leans over and kisses her shoulder. The smell of her body is intoxicating. She stirs, clears her throat, and then moves away from him.

He whispers, 'I didn't tell you how close that tiger got to eating me.'

There is no answer. Doesn't she care?

'Margaret!'

'Oh, Wallace, I'm tired. Tell me in the morning.'

'It is morning.'

Her breathing is even and slow but he isn't fooled. She isn't asleep.

'Darling, come to me.'

He understands her silence to be an invitation. Fully aroused, he wastes no time, enters her and climaxes immediately. It has been so long, travelling in the hills and not a woman in sight. He hadn't meant to grip her arms so tightly but it is only natural: a man's desire has to be satisfied after so long a time away.

He dozes, his arm flung out on the counterpane. Beside him, Margaret curls up near to the edge of the bed and stares at the brightening window. She is no longer the woman Wallace McKay married. If she tried to explain, he wouldn't understood. When he touches her, she feels nothing. How could he know what she has been through? How could any man? Night after night, lying awake, her face wet with tears. It took her all her strength to visit the cemetery and when she got there, she sat on a bench, in the shade of a eucalyptus tree, and whispered to the baby. An hour passed – maybe two – without her realising it. Afterwards, she couldn't recall one word she had said. Other visitors in the cemetery took no notice of her. Among the gravestones, a white-haired woman in mourning dress and muttering prayers is a commonplace sight.

One day, she visited the cemetery and sat down in her usual place under the eucalyptus. Above her head, leaves rustled, birds sang. As if for the first time, she heard them. She did not speak. An observer wouldn't have seen any difference, and yet Margaret was acutely aware of the shift inside her.

Where her heart once was, there was now a void.

X

BELFAST 1919

'I am so sorry about the wee wean,' Alice Poots whispers when they embrace.

Margaret purses her lips and sweeps on into the house, the three little girls in tow. A coldness lodges in her bones. Nothing matters. She wanted to be back in Ireland in order to revel in everyday things: to sit in Alice's warm kitchen. Now that she is here, she and her friend are separated, it seems to her, by a curtain of fog. To be here. Or there. Where is home exactly? When she is in Shillong, she wants to be in Ireland, and yet in Ireland she is a foreigner.

'I am glad you're home,' Alice takes her coat and hat to hang in the closet under the stairs. 'I've been worried sick about you. So far away and the times we've lived through. The war and that terrible business in Dublin, all over now, thank the Lord.'

Margaret is brisk. 'I'll only be in Ireland long enough to settle the children in school.'

Growing up, they were inseparable: Margaret, her sister Molly and their friend Alice Poots. Molly, a Wren, is still billeted in Grimsby. Coming home, Margaret has longed for the old, familiar sights: the Dublin coastline rising to welcome her, the streets, clean and firm underfoot, the glinting glass cases in shop windows, the counter girls talking in soft city accents, electric lights burning on a winter's evening, fresh cream buns for afternoon tea and braised beef for dinner.

The maid had gone out for the messages so the two women sit in the kitchen and talk while the children play outside. In the pantry, there are neat rows of jam and tins of meat. The old sink in the scullery has been replaced with a metal one. Margaret puts her cup down on the table.

'Oh Lord, I needed that,' she says. 'The Belfast train is so stuffy.'

'Another cup?'

'Please. You know I miss our Irish tea. Did you ever think? Stuck in the middle of Assam with acres of tea all around.'

Here it is black as tar with creamy milk swirling at the rim. Sugary. Just the way she likes it.

After tea, Margaret duly admires everything, but when they go into the parlour, her heart sinks. Once it was a room full of promise, smelling of fresh paint and new curtains. The delight of two newlyweds. Now the parlour is pokey, not how she remembers it. So much has changed, Margaret thinks. And I have changed most of all.

There is pity in Alice's eyes. 'You look tired, dear.'

Margaret grimaces. Tired means old. Her white hair is terribly ageing. She could be taken for her mother these days. Poor mother who is buried in Moneyreagh churchyard.

'I must call to the old house.' Even if her father has no desire to see her, she is obliged to go for Jane's sake. Unlike her spinster sister, Margaret enjoys a freedom that is not to be underestimated. Her world has opened wide and, in a faraway country, she has made a home.

Meanwhile changes, small and big, have taken place. Alice's parlour has grown cramped. The sight of Sackville Street bombed to rubble and more Union Jacks flying than ever before, has enraged her. As she visits family and friends, she senses that deep in the landscape something is shuddering awake. That terrible business in Dublin, she is certain, is not over. The newspapers are full of the success of Sinn Féin in the general election. The Great War is already fading into history and, whether in a dream or in reality, there is a David and Goliath struggle emerging. The British Empire on one side, a motley crew of naysayers on the other. Well, she knows which side she is on.

'How exciting it must have been for you, Alice!'

'What do you mean?'

'To cast your first vote. What was it like?'

The other woman gives her a sidelong glance.

'Oh, Alice, how could you not?'

There is no reply.

'To think how women struggled to get you the vote. I'd have given my eye teeth ...'

Alice looks cross. 'Well, I didn't, so there.'

'While I was stuck in India you were free to vote and you chose not to.'

'Heavens, dear, keep your hair on.'

Margaret's voice rises. 'I can't believe it.'

The other woman straightens up. 'I wouldn't have voted for thon rebels anyway. Not when I think of the men who fought and died.'

'Aye, Irishmen dying for the rights of any small nation except their own one.'

Alice bridles. 'Those men made their sacrifice while your Wallace was far away.'

Margaret doesn't rise to the bait.

'Don't you see, Alice?' she declares. 'Our small nation is being oppressed by a foreign government.'

There was a time when Alice was afraid of Margaret's temper, when she would have acquiesced to anything in order to avoid a row, but she is a married woman in her own right now, and the two of them are sitting in her kitchen which, even though she says it only to herself, looks particularly cheery with the copper pots brightly polished and the little bunch of violets Margaret has brought gracing the Waterford vase that belongs in the parlour.

'Ach, Margaret,' Alice says, covering her mouth in a fit of giggles, 'if I didn't know better, I'd say you were a Sinn Féiner. These days a body could be locked up for speaking like that.'

Margaret slaps the table with her fists. The violets shiver. 'And if I didn't know better I'd say you were a lickspittle for the Orange.'

'Now you're just being mean.'

Margaret chews on her lip. When they have so little time together why must Alice be so provoking? But her friend refuses to take offence. There is no point. Poor Margaret has always had a bad temper and will never change. What cannot be cured must be endured. Thankfully the little girls are a delight, well-mannered and polite, unlike their mother, she thinks but does not say.

'When you have the children settled will you stay on in Dublin for a while?'

Margaret busies herself with her purse and gloves. 'I'll return to India as soon as I can get a passage from Southampton. I don't want to leave Wallace for too long.'

She is surprised how much she misses him. He swims up out of the oceans that keep them apart and stands before her, looking his most serious self. It won't be long now. The pieces are falling into place. Mr and Mrs Bennington at Brookfield are exactly as she imagined them: typical Quaker folk who made her feel welcome. The other children already in their care looked content: the girls in well-pressed pinafores and stiff-plaited hair, the boys in woollen suits. She liked the well-ordered school with its big windows overlooking the garden. Next door, the Friends' Meeting House is a timbered room, plain and unadorned. No fancy frills about it, she writes to Wallace, a perfect place for private prayer.

'I'm bringing Alexandra to stay with the McKays once I have settled the two older girls at school.'

'Won't you miss them when you go back, Margaret?'

'We'll get home on leave but it's better that the girls are safe and well here. That is the most important thing.'

'Oh, my dear ...'

Margaret is unflinching. 'It's getting dark. I'll call in the girls for I must be off. Thank you, Alice. It was a lovely day, and for the tea.'

When Margaret arrives at her mother-in-law's house, she keeps a firm hold of Alexandra's hand. She is taken aback by the run-down air of the farmhouse at Seacon, the mould stains on the walls, the drain pipes weeping rust and at the front door, the old stone flags are covered in mud. She will have to tell Wallace how his family is living. The sooner the new house is built the better.

Eliza McKay, wearing widow's black, is waiting at the open door. She looks frail, as thin as a heron.

'I am sorry for your loss, Mrs McKay.'

Her mother-in-law is impatient. 'How is Wallace? Is he looking after himself?'

Margaret does not want the conversation to veer towards the baby's death, so she talks about the bungalow and the golf club in Shillong. Nothing she says makes any difference: her mother-in-law sits in her rocking chair, looking gloomy. Margaret perches on the kitchen bench and secretly yearns to escape the stale smell of clothes drying over the range. Surely Mrs McKay could open up the parlour for her visit?

'We have such a good life in Shillong.'

The old woman rocks back and forth, wringing her hands, wiping her eyes with her apron. Alexandra looks on, appalled.

'Mummy.' She tugs at her mother's sleeve but Margaret shushes her.

'Really, Mrs McKay, don't be worrying. Wallace is making his way in the world.'

Eliza's expression is shadowed with pain. 'When will he come and visit me?'

Is this why we have children, Margaret wonders, so they can grow up and break our hearts by leaving? She is not a sentimentalist: she has settled Maggie and Elizabeth at the Quaker school, although saying goodbye was harder than she expected. She steeled herself. *It is for the best ...* She could not endure any more suffering. Her girls are safe in Ireland, that is the most important thing. They are mature enough, she consoled herself, and they have each other. All the same, she is dismayed when her sister-in-law Anna rushes into the kitchen and spins her little niece around, saying, 'Come along, Alexa, we'll go and see the chickens,' and the child, her sturdy feet in her new boots, goes so happily out into the yard. The child's name is Alexandra, Margaret wants to say but she is conscious that her mother-in-law is watching her. She feels a drag under her breast. How long will it be before she sees her children again? She bites her lip. She must not cry, not for all the tea in India.

'We will both come to visit, I promise,' she says as she puts on her coat and fixes her hat, 'whenever Wallace has leave. I have to catch the evening train so I'll go and say goodbye to Alexandra.'

Without a word, Eliza McKay stands up and rattles the kettle on the range with such force that droplets of water spray out and land, hissing, on the hot surface.

That night, for the first and only time, Alexandra cries for her mother. Anna lies down beside her in the bed and, twirling one of her ringlets around her finger, sings a lullaby until the little girl falls asleep.

'Come downstairs, daughter, and get warm,' Eliza calls from the kitchen. Finger to her lips, Anna obeys. Mother and daughter sit by the range and talk into the night. The death of the old man has shrouded the farmhouse in gloom for long enough: the arrival of the child lightens everything. The two women often disagree but they are united on one thing.

'There's not a whit of human kindness in thon woman that married our Wallace. To leave a wean, only four years old and walk away.'

'And in such a hurry to go stravaiging across the world,' Anna says, 'that she hardly said a word to me.'

'Would you say,' her mother's look is mischievous, 'that is a blessing?'

XI

A devil, perched in his big toe, keeps Wallace awake during the night. The day before, after the accident happened, he removed his boot and stocking and examined his foot. A bit bruised and cut, that was all. He should have more sense, letting a half-broken gelding get the better of him. Later, during the night, he is wide awake and on edge. Every few seconds, a flash of pain scuds through his body. Quinine would do the trick but he doesn't have any, and old Dr Hamilton is worse than useless, bumbling around like an old fool. Margaret would know what to do but she is in Ireland. Meanwhile Wallace is spancelled by an inflamed toe. It is ridiculous.

In the morning his foot is so swollen he sits at the breakfast table, with a slipper on the injured foot, a shoe on the other. When Baia comes in and puts down a plate of scrambled eggs, she catches sight of his feet.

'Babu,' she giggles, 'your shoes are not correct.'

'It's not a laughing matter.'

Ever since Margaret left, Baia has become quite fresh with him. She still treats him with deference but there is a discernible change in her manner. Little touches, a vase of flowers on the table, his bed warmed with a hot water bottle, her face brightening when he tells her about his day. There is no one else to talk to except the chaps in the club, who are only interested in playing golf and swilling gin. When he joins them at the bar he never fails to buy his round but it is awkward to end up, every night, being the only sober man in the place. With the children and Margaret gone, he spends much of his time alone. I will go to the club, he decides. Someone there will sort me out.

Baia kneels down to get a better look. He flinches when she touches the swelling. She is no longer his servant, he decides, she is his keeper.

'I'll go later to the club. They will sort a fellow out.'

'The club is not open on Sunday.'

Sunday. Lord, he forgot. Now he's facing into another sleepless night. He could call on Lavinia Frobisher for assistance but his spirit shrivels at the thought. She could make his life a misery. With half a chance, she would have moved in after Margaret left: every day bringing little parcels of food and sitting for hours prattling, until he wanted to boot her out the door. She reminds him of a leech slithering up inside his trouser leg. Of course, he is polite, but some hint of his revulsion must have got through to her. He is relieved when her visits lessen and then stop. Now, whenever they meet at the club, she is chilly towards him.

Baia stands up. 'You come with me, babu.'

Wallace is taken aback. I will do no such thing, little madam, he is about to say but when she proposes that they go to the Unitarian church, he is intrigued. Mr Kissor Singh will be able to help him, she is certain; he is known throughout Shillong for his cures. Wallace has never met Kissor Singh although he is aware that he has quite a following among the Khasi people. The idea of a man who came independently to an enlightened view of the world appeals to him. Out of the blue, here is an opportunity to meet the Unitarian minister. What harm could it do? He is in no condition to refuse Baia, even if she was being too bossy for her own good.

'After I finish my breakfast, go and hire me a tonga.' Aye, he thinks, that was said in a suitably crushing tone.

Initially the ayah trots behind the tonga, panting in her effort to keep up. Wallace orders to driver to stop. He leans out. 'Get in, Baia.'

She climbs up onto the seat beside him. Although there is room for only two people she manages to nestle in so neatly that their bodies do not touch. She doesn't take up any more space than a child, Wallace thinks, with her arms crossed tightly across her breast, her little feet tucked under her apron. Eventually they arrive in a part of the town that is unfamiliar to him. Streets undulate in a maze of one-roomed thatched houses. Baia directs the driver to hurry or they will miss the end of the service and Mr Singh will be gone. Wallace doesn't say a word. If Margaret could see him now, she would have laughed at him. *Led through the nose,* but, in a way, he finds it exciting to be rushing through the streets to God knows where.

Their destination is a white-washed building set in a courtyard. As they step down from the tonga, they are met by the sound of singing from inside the church. The words are unrecognisable but the music speaks to him. *'Abide with me,'* he says loudly but Baia isn't listening as she leads him into the back of the church. The interior is simple: rough walls, an earthen floor, and no seating. At the far end of the church, under a narrow window, the Khasi minister stands. When the singing dies away, he addresses the congregation. *Amen,* they answer and the service comes to an end.

Kissor Singh turns out to be a short, stocky man with a strong face, flat cheekbones, a wide mouth and luxuriant moustache. Someone – was it the Methodist minister Mr Peacock? – said that the Khasi looks like a country gardener who grows the best vegetables for miles around.

Without thinking, Wallace says, 'I believe we dig with the same foot.'

Mystified, the minister turns to Baia. She shakes her head.

'I am Unitarian too, I mean.'

Kissor Singh smiles.

Inside Wallace's slipper, the devil has started up again, gnawing savagely.

He is impatient. 'Baia, tell him why I'm here.'

The minister leads them into a windowless room in an annexe to the church. Through the doorway a shaft of daylight reveals a low bench. He invites Wallace to sit down and remove his slipper. In silence, he examines the offending foot. When he stands up, Kissor Singh speaks to Baia. Without any explanation, he slips out of the room with the ayah in his wake.

'Wait to have tea, babu,' she says on her way out.

Tea! Wallace doesn't want tea; he doesn't want to be there at all. The whole thing is a wild goose chase. He should have known better. He will call on Dr Hamilton and try to coax a batch of quinine out of him. He glowers at his foot.

When Kissor Singh re-enters he is carrying two steaming bowls which he places on the earthen floor. He kneels down and takes Wallace's foot onto his knee. He speaks to Baia who has followed him into the room. She puts down the tray she is carrying.

'He says it will hurt now.'

Whatever Wallace expected, it wasn't to have his foot scalded by an oily concoction being applied by two strong, brown hands. 'Damnation,' he hisses between his clenched teeth. Catching Baia's eye, he realises that the little minx is laughing at him.

Blushing, she presents him with a cup of tea. A peace offering. The tea is sweet and strong. He sits back on the bench and rests his back against the wall. Everything around him slows: the oil, gradually cooling, Kissor Singh massaging his foot now with measured strokes. Lulled by the sensation of the minister's fingers kneading his skin, Wallace closes his eyes. *Oh, my dear Margaret, I miss you so much.*

Kissor Singh wipes away the oil with a palm cloth and then takes a handful of thick paste from the other bowl. Carefully he slathers the foot with paste until it is encased in a doughy covering. The greyish paste looked familiar to Wallace. Of course, it is a poultice, not much different from the one his mother prepared to cure a boil.

Wallace is surprised when Kissor Singh says in English. 'You and I must wait now. It will draw out the sickness. When you go home Baia will do this for three days, five times a day.'

'Good Lord, is that really necessary?'

'Very necessary.'

A silence falls in the dusky room. When Kissor Singh speaks again, he is hesitant. 'May we talk while we wait?'

'Of course.'

'You have come to my church. Now I would like to hear about your church.'

Immediately the Dublin church rises up to meet him: its ashlar walls and stained glass windows; its air of territorial certainty. There was a time when congregations had suffered obloquy, even persecution. They were called king killers. Now Unitarians have come into their own. The generosity of benefactors built a church fine enough to match their standing in society. Wallace is proud of the Dublin congregation, although, sitting in a bare room being attended to by this stranger, he isn't sure if he can explain why. He picks a pebble up from the earthen floor and rolls it around in his hand.

'Our minister is a wise man, no more than yourself,' he says. 'He told us to remember three things. Firstly, to be tolerant of the beliefs of others. Secondly, that other people who are just as clever or conscientious as ourselves hold different opinions to ours. Thirdly, that Jesus did not leave any formalised doctrine or creed behind him.'

Kissor Singh nods. 'Ah yes. "Let every man be persuaded in his own mind."'

Wallace starts up in surprise. 'Those very same words are written on the wall of the Unitarian church in Ballymoney, where I grew up,' he says. 'How extraordinary!'

Let every man ... It is a touchstone: the principle of individual conscience that has guided him throughout his life. This is how the world can amaze. The town of Shillong is built on a clear division: Europeans in one quarter, the natives in another. In his restlessness, Wallace has travelled halfway across the globe, only to discover that the churches of Ballymoney and Shillong are built on common ground.

XII

How did it happen? It is a mystery: how he has entered into a carnal paradise where there is no right or wrong.

No, that isn't true.

He is a moral man who, lonely and vulnerable, has been tempted beyond endurance, by the allurement of Eve.

No, that isn't true either.

Wallace is not a man to apportion blame unfairly. First and foremost, he is a man of reason who understands human nature. The urge that overwhelms a man of common sense is a necessary one: it is the urge, after all, that secures the future of the human race. He has made his choice, his body and hers sliding together. 'Baia ...' he hears himself groan as he penetrates deep inside her. Her short legs twined around his long ones. Her skin smelling of sandalwood, her little breasts as familiar to him as if she was always there, as if she is a part of him. In the darkness, with a strange woman in his bed, he understands what it means to feel alive. It is shameful, yes, but it is true.

Laughter is his undoing and, in the candlelight, her fingers tickling the instep of his foot. That first night she comes into his bedroom, carrying two bowls, and wakes him out of a deep sleep.

'Babu,' she murmurs as she folds back the sheet to uncover his foot.

She doesn't use hot oil as Kissor Singh did. The liquid dripping onto his skin is cool, her fingers are firm and gentle as she works. When she is finished massaging in the oil, she stands up and smooths down her apron. Even in the gloom, her smile is radiant.

'Big toe,' she giggles. 'Big, big toe.'

In fact, the swelling has subsided, somewhat. The treatment is working.

'Not that big,' he says. 'It's the way I'm built.'

She lifts up her foot to be alongside his. He sits up in the bed to take a look. Her foot and his, side by side, make an incongruous sight, as if they belong to different species. A bubble of laughter rises in his throat.

She crouches down at the side of the bed and begins to spread the poultice on his foot. He lies back on the pillows, a languor seeping through his body. He has forgotten what a woman's touch feels like. Baia's delicate hand on the sole of his foot is a reminder. How pleasurable it is. So close in the night, the two of them form a tableau in his mind of a servant kneeling before a master who is stretched out, a wounded soldier on a litter. He feels himself grow hard at the thought of their coming together, her childlike ease enveloping him and making him whole again. His body rising up, renewed.

Who kissed who first? He can't remember. There are so many kisses: long and passionate ones; others light and playful. Without a word, she slips out of her robe and reaches into his embrace.

It has been too long ...

During the day he keeps himself busy. He leaves the running of the household to the servants and often hears Baia, her voice high and furious, arguing with the cook in the kitchen, but he is aware of their quarrels at one remove, through an open door, or by a window while he sits at his desk, an inane grin on his face, revelling in the secret life they now share while, at the same time, asking himself, how did it happen?

After the dinner plates have been cleared away and the lamps lit, he sits in his bedroom, pretending to read until he hears her footsteps in the corridor. Then he springs out of his chair and goes to open the door. Sometimes, she moves so quietly, like an owl flitting through the shadows, that she is standing in the room before he sees her. On the night before he sets out on an inspection tour, she comes to his bedroom as usual. After they make love, he stretches out in the bed and, although he is wide awake, closes his eyes. He has a long day ahead, he tells her, and needs to rest. It is her custom to wait until he falls asleep and then to slip quietly out of the bed. To his dismay, this night she wants to talk. He has come to know every nook and crevice of her body and yet *who* she is does not interest him. She is Baia, that is all he knows or cares about, but there is no stopping her. With growing impatience, he listens while she speaks about her life. Her father is dead, her sick mother depends on the wage she brings home.

'Bon, my uncle is a good man,' she says, 'He helps us too.'

Wallace's unease mushrooms into panic. The spectre of Margaret is always at the back of his mind. *A degenerate*, he called Malcolm Frobisher when he took a native woman to his bed. Now he is the one balancing on a precipice of disgrace. How much worse can it get? Bon is Baia's uncle. Maybe the cook and the gardener are too. Maybe he is surrounded by her relatives. This madness must stop now. He is going away in the morning and when he returns,

Wallace says, she is not to come to his bedroom again. His voice is laden with contempt. For her, yes, but contempt for himself most of all.

'Do you understand what I'm saying? It is finished.'

Will she obey him? Steeling himself, he thinks, she *must*. Without saying a word, she slips out of the bed, puts on her robe and disappears as discreetly as she came in.

At daybreak, Bon brings the horses around to the front of the bungalow, and the two men set out. Wallace is relieved that Baia doesn't come onto the veranda to say goodbye in the way she usually does. He is certain she won't talk: her position in the household depends on her silence. As for him, he is heading into the forests that cover the Meghalaya hills, mile upon mile, all the way to Burma. Bon rides up ahead, his rifle cocked at the ready, his face impassive. Wallace follows with hunched shoulders, wearing his guilt like an old saturated coat. Before long, his mood lightens and he straightens up in the saddle. All he has to do is to keep on going, and soon, for the first time in weeks, he will be a free man.

Miss Barr's invitation had sounded incongruously prim on the last time they met in Shillong. As if she were asking him to join her for afternoon tea. Please do call in, if you're passing ...

Wallace decides to take Miss Barr at her word. It makes sense to break his journey, to stay for a night and rest the horses. First they travel in deep forests, then they arrive in a clearing where a number of huts are huddled together. He admires Miss Barr. She has an honesty that appeals to him and an intelligence that makes for good conversation. All the same, he is shocked when he sees that her hut is as dishevelled as the rest. She makes a peculiar sight, dressed like a native, standing in her doorway and madly waving as he and Bon ride into the clearing.

'It is good to see you, Miss Barr,' he says and means it.

'Oh, Mr McKay, it is a great pleasure to see you. You can tell me all your news and then I'll tell you mine,' she says as she takes hold of the horse's bridle. 'I can only offer you some local rice and a few vegetables. It is plain fare but it is all the people have here. I must warn you that, in the past, I've found the food difficult to eat.'

'It will be a pleasure.'

She chuckles. 'It is worse by far to eat alone.'

When Wallace produces some white rice and vegetables out of the saddle bag she claps her hands, 'Dear Lord, now we will have a feast. There's no cutlery, I'm afraid. Here we eat the Khasi way.'

After they have eaten, they sit at the fire outside her hut and talk. Above, the great canopy of trees hides the stars. The sounds of animals shifting in the undergrowth and the fire crackling make a backdrop to their conversation. She tells him that she hopes to embark on the building of a school for local children, as soon as the church in England will sanction payment. Her face is vivid with excitement. If the money comes in time, she will start before the rainy season. They talk about religion, politics, the character of the Khasi, the future of India, her interest in education, his views on the latest tea-planting techniques. He is slow to ask her any intimate questions, but curiosity wins out in the end.

'How on earth do you live like this?'

'I can't imagine living any other way,' she says. 'You have not lived until you have done something for someone who can never repay you.'

Wallace smiles in recognition. 'Bunyan says, of course. *A Pilgrim's Progress*. No, I tell a lie: it's a line from a poem of his.'

For a moment her round face puckers. 'I love the outdoors. I'm just back from a tour into the hills with the Khasis.'

Miss Barr, as his mother might say, is one brave wee woman. He feels a pang of envy. Apart from his visits to the tea gardens, his life is tame by comparison.

He persists. 'But how can you bear the solitude?'

'Of course, it was lonely, at the start. The first tour I went on, the Khasis insisted on carrying white rice and English vegetables for me. I had a tussle to persuade my guide to let me carry my own rucksack. This time was better: I was eating the coarse rice they eat and any vegetables that happened to be available, cooked by the woman who prepared the food for the rest of the party. When we approached a new village, a mass of curious brown faces came thronging around, and my heart almost failed me. Now, wherever we go, there are familiar faces, many with names attached, and I can talk enough to make myself understood. This time even the babies are less uncompromisingly hostile.'

Stifling a yawn, she throws a stick on the fire. He watches the sparks explode into the night air. Could he live the life she has chosen, without comfort, books, family or friends? The life of a true missionary, although she has rejected that description for herself. Dreamily, she continues, as if she has forgotten he is there. Living alone, he realises, can make a body garrulous.

'At mealtimes, I dined in solitary state. I saw my Khasi companions praying before their simple meal and thought that if I couldn't eat with them I was, to them, a foreigner and as long as I was that I was one apart. I couldn't help them as I wanted to. Then, suddenly, I heard one of the women say, *Mem, come and eat with us.* Had she read my thoughts, I don't know but even though I had already eaten, I took up her invitation. I joined the circle and from then on, I was one of the family.'

One of the family. Miss Barr is too engrossed in her story to notice his surprise.

He is polite. 'So you have settled in.'

She brushes his comment aside. 'I have dispensed entirely with knives and forks, and, furthermore, I hope never to be expected to use them again among the Khasis. And what is more,' her eyes gleam. 'I know the joy of communion as never before in my life.'

Joy ... The word sings in his head.

Miss Barr has stayed true to a higher purpose. By choosing the Khasis to be her family, she has found happiness. Such is the prize of her pilgrim's progress through tiger-infested forests, dangerous rivers, the enmity of strangers. And what has *he* done? Sick with shame, Wallace contemplates the answer. It coils, snake-like, inside his consciousness: he has betrayed his wife with a Khasi woman. He shrinks from the memory. What if he confesses his sin to Miss Barr, kneels down before her, beating his breast? He grimaces. It is a ridiculous idea, and unworthy of a man of his intelligence, so he teases her instead. Looking around at the bamboo huts, the tethered goat at her door, he says, 'I see, Miss Barr, that you have reached your celestial city.'

'Ah, quit your nonsense.'

'You know you could write a book, except someone else already has.'

She cackles with delight, leans forward to prod him with a stick. Her playfulness lifts his mood. They are like two boys, sitting at a campfire in the middle of nowhere, telling stories and larking about. Eventually, with reluctance, she stands up and spreads her hands down over her apron. 'You have an early start.'

'And a long way to travel.'

She looks anxious. 'Are you sure you're going to be alright sleeping here?'

'I shall lie down at the door of your hut and protect you from danger.'

'I see,' she says, her expression solemn. 'And tell me now, Mr McKay, who is going to protect you from danger?'

As if, he thinks, she has seen into my soul.

He is glad to be lying in his bedroll under the trees while, beneath him, their roots spread through the earth. That day he crossed a bridge made up of the roots of fig trees, woven together by local Khasis and marvelled at their ingenuity. Timbers rot and break in the wet climate, but a bridge of living roots endures. There is a lesson to be learnt: in striving to be strong, he must use his brain as well as his brawn. To prevail, self-discipline is needed. With Margaret coming back to him, they can start afresh. Maybe even have another baby. He turns onto his back and stares up at the sky. Being in the company of Miss Barr has given him peace of mind. She is a good egg not that she would thank him for saying so. He is protected from danger: only a few feet away from him Bon is curled up in his bedroll and alert, even in slumber, to any threats. Wallace turns onto his side, his hand seeking comfort between his legs. Desire washes through him as he feels himself grow hard. Baia ... Her naked body straddling his, her tongue moving in his mouth. Will he never be free? His hand jerking until he comes at last and is released from her memory. Above him, the trees are stirring. A mynah bird calls and, in the darkness, Bon groans in his sleep.

Wallace lifts his head from the microscope and looks at the tea planter beside him.

'A common problem: *Rosellina Arcuata* or, as it is better known, root rot.'

'Bloody hell, what am I going to do?'

Mark Wakefield's chubby face and helpless air are, in their own way, endearing. There is nothing Wallace enjoys more than teaching others about the cultivation of tea, and Mark is an eager student. Tea planters, Wallace has found, are made up of two groups: those who are glad to see him and those who are vitriolic at what they see as intrusion by the company. Damn pen pushers, what do they know? They see him as the enemy, a view reinforced when he refuses to join them in their drinking bouts. Mark Wakefield belongs to the first group. Wallace takes to him immediately. The two men spend long hours in the gardens and factory. The laboratory Mark has built is rudimentary but Wallace understands its possibilities. He talks to the planter about tea types, diseases, pests. In response, words tumble out of Mark's mouth: questions and comments, stray profanities. Wallace is patient. There is always something to learn from the men in the field. It isn't so long since he was one himself. As an agricultural adviser, his learning is superior. He reads the latest research and takes pride in his reservoir of knowledge. His confidence has grown since his early days in India. Tea has become a passion. He has bought a camera and keeps a record of the various diseases of tea plants. One day he might publish a book. Leaving Frobisher's tea garden and striking out on his own – it was the best decision he ever made.

By the end of the tour, he has spent ten weeks visiting various tea gardens. With relief, he and Bon turn for home. He is eager to have a decent hot bath and a shave, to read the newspapers, to pick up the threads of his life. He is stronger, fitter, leaner than he has ever been. Mark

Wakefield pumping his hand, saying *Dash it all, I can't thank you enough*. Yes, he has earned the right to be satisfied with himself. Wallace envisages his desk in the bungalow piled with correspondence, imagines fresh tonic water and lime in a cut glass tumbler waiting for him in the club, the chaps gathering for dinner. For once, he will have stories to tell instead of sitting like a dummy while they do the talking. He envisages dreamless nights between linen sheets and eating scrambled eggs for breakfast with a silver fork. He wishes for nothing more than to have his life back, and the prospect of travelling down river in the spring to meet Margaret when her ship docks in Calcutta.

The scene unfolds just as he imagined: the bungalow, the jacaranda tree in the garden, his clean bed and a hearty breakfast. On his second day at home, there is a knock on the door. What a handsome man, he thinks at the sight of Bon's sleek bald head and strong shoulders, his crisp, white tunic. What can his guide possibly want, surely not to play on his generosity? For a native, the man is better paid than most.

'What is it?' he barks.

Never in a hundred years could he have envisaged what Bon has come to tell him: that Baia is expecting a child and that the child is his.

XIII

In Calcutta, everything in the hotel bedroom is redolent of luxury: lotus petals float in brass bowls, a fine silk counterpane, the four-poster bed, the tasselled rugs on a marble floor. While Margaret changes into her new blue dress, Wallace waits. He comes to stand behind her when she sits down at the dressing table. Sliding the tie around his neck, his face contorts as he struggles to get the bow to lie straight while Margaret fastens her hair with tortoiseshell combs.

'Let me help you.'

She turns, takes the ends of the tie and arranges them into a neat, flat bow. He doesn't even say thank you. What is wrong with him? she wonders. His discourtesy reopens a wound. It is inexcusable to have made the decision without her say-so.

'Why on earth did you let Baia go?'

He cowers before the remembrance of Baia at the doorway, small and smiling. Her belly swollen inside her servant's apron.

'Baia,' Wallace pauses, 'was untrustworthy.'

The figure vanishes. He breaks out in a sweat; fingers scrabble at his tie.

Judas.

Oblivious, Margaret smiles at their reflection in the mirror.

'How handsome you are,' she says.

He knows she is waiting for a compliment in return. She sighs and, gazing into the mirror, says, 'What a handsome couple we make.'

Agitated, he finds the bow tie unravelling in his hands. When she sees what he has done, she flies into a rage. 'For heaven's sake, what has got into you, Wallace? Can't you just leave it be?'

She stands up and grips the tie around his neck. He steps back. Is she about to choke him? He wouldn't put it past her, if she ever found out.

'Stand still!'

Even as she harangues him, her fingers work to make a bow again. He lets her anger seep into him. It is a welcome release.

They are staying in the Tollygunge Hotel for a fortnight before leaving for Shillong. Margaret had so looked forward to their being together after their months' separation, and yet when it is just the two of them he withdraws into himself and she can't reach him. From the moment she saw him standing out of the crowd on the quay as her ship docked, she knew something was wrong. He looked so morose and thin. Was he ill?

'No, not at all.'

'You don't seem very pleased to see me.'

'Of course I am, dear.'

A desultory peck on her cheek. Then he fussed over the trunks, refusing to catch her eye. Maybe she has been away too long. She must be patient, although patience doesn't come easily to her. She can't bear to see anyone in a sulk. Wallace has temporarily lost his way, she decides. Nothing a few weeks of comfort and good food won't fix, but, as the days pass, nothing changes except his frantic need to be with other people.

In company, he who is usually shy becomes loquacious: talking to all and sundry, planning bridge parties and excursions. His newfound sociability dismays her. Until now, making new friends has been up to her. The hotel is humming with guests: tea planters with their wives, army officers, and company men bent on making money. In the afternoons the residents thin out: some go to the golf course, others to their bedrooms to rest.

In the grand hall the only sound is the thump of the punka wallahs' fans. Wallace goes to the library to write letters and Margaret is left to amuse herself. She sits on a rattan chair on the veranda, an unopened letter beside her on a silver-topped table. A letter from home is usually a pleasure, particularly now that she is stuck in the Tollygunge and dying of boredom. She yearns to be up in the hills in Shillong where there is familiar company, Mrs Frobisher and the others, good for a few rubbers of bridge. When the time comes to leave Shillong, she knows that a part of her will be left behind. It is inexplicable, her baby is dead while her father is alive and penned up in his bed, causing havoc.

She lifts the envelope onto her lap and feels a chill, despite the heat. If anything has happened, there would be a black border on the envelope. Funny to think of her father brought low in the cause of Home Rule. To suffer for one's beliefs, all the same, even if it was by falling off a bicycle while canvassing for votes, does have a hint of grandeur about it.

When Margaret was in Ireland, she left the visit to his farmhouse until last. She found her childhood home unchanged, although most of the family had gone away. The only ones left were her younger sister Jane and their invalid father.

Jane's gaze was all-knowing when she greeted her.

'Aha,' she said. 'India suits you.'

Yes, it does, Margaret thought with surprise. In Shillong she is her own woman. Soon she will be free of ties, returning to Wallace without the children. The prospect was tantalising. What had Jane to look forward to, shackled to a bellowing wreck of an old man?

'How are you coping?'

'He has his good days. There are other times when I fear for my life.'

'How dreadful for you.'

A fly hovered between them. Jane swatted it away. 'What can I do?'

'There must be something.'

The fly buzzed, then settled on the window frame.

'He could be sent to the asylum,' Margaret said.

'I couldn't do that to Daddy. No matter how bad he is.'

'But you can't go on like this.'

'Well, I won't do it,' Jane stood up and squashed the fly with her closed fist.

Margaret sighed. 'I won't be able to help you when I am halfway across the world.'

'Don't you see?' Jane's eyes blackened as she whirled round. 'I couldn't bear the shame of it.'

Margaret blew out her cheeks. 'I don't care one bit what the neighbours think.'

'Ach, easy for you to say. You're never here.' There was no animosity in her sister's voice as she looked down at the dead fly on the window sill. 'I think of you sometimes, so far away you could be living on the moon. When you brought Wallace here for the first time, the two of you seemed so different I couldn't imagine you being happy with him. Wallace always polite, chilly even, while you have the Minnis temper. Ice and fire, you are.'

Margaret smiled. 'How romantic.'

Jane looked at her vaguely. 'I suppose opposites do attract.'

'Jane, what are you going to do?'

Her sister shook her head.

'Have you thought about the future at all?'

'The future! There is no future here in Ulster.' Jane spat venomously into the fire. 'Mr William Carson has us back in 1690 and people around too thran to see it.'

Margaret sighed. Their dream of Home Rule was in ruins. As children they talked about the future. They were full of excitement when Mr Parnell had visited the manse at Moneyreagh. Not even a glimpse of him did they have, but the mere idea of him nearby meant somehow that Home Rule was inevitable.

'I just want to help.' It was very difficult, Margaret thought, to make herself understood.

'Well, you can,' Jane's voice dropped to a whisper. 'I heard tell of a woman in Newry.'

Margaret was met with a look of such innocence in her sister's face she was disarmed.

'Is she a nurse?'

'Of a kind.'

'Go on. I'm listening.'

'I've been told ...'

'For heaven's sake, what have you been told?'

Jane took her time, smoothed down the pockets in her dress, touched her hair. Then, in a rush. 'She is a woman that gets rid of unwanted parents.'

'What?'

Her sister sat, straight-backed, the very picture of respectability. As if making polite conversation, she added, 'I hear she charges an amount and gives you the medicine to administer. If you want her to do it, she charges more. Five pounds I believe.'

Had her sister lost her mind?

'I'm saying nothing mind. It is good to know these things, that's all.' Jane's tone was flat. 'Otherwise, I might go mad too.'

From the bedroom, a strangled shriek reverberated through the house. The two women fell silent, listening while the clamour got louder.

Jane sighed. 'Daddy wants his tea.'

As she prepared to leave, Margaret buttoned up her gloves and fixed her hat before the pier glass. Her reflection was blurred in the dim light. Who was she to judge? The old man did not recognise her, his own daughter. Her presence had driven his crazed mind into a turmoil. She took a deep breath: soon she would be aboard ship and away from it all. On the front step, Jane gave her a perfunctory kiss. Margaret was about to walk away when she turned back, and pulled her sister to her with such force that their cheekbones collided.

'Write to me if you need money, Jane,' she whispered. 'You will have it, I promise, all you have to do is ask.'

Now Margaret opens the envelope with trepidation, but the letter contains nothing by way of news except that Jane sold all the chickens to pay for the new roof on the barn. Their father is just the same: no better and no worse. She lets the letter fall in her lap. The punka wallah is dozing. The air is a dead weight. Her expectations have turned to dust. She feels useless. She has always known how to get around Wallace in the past. A little cajoling goes a long way, particularly when it is aimed at his sense of decency. Now she is powerless: yearning for the safety of his embrace while she is incapable of reaching across the expanse between them. He knows she doesn't want another child. How could he put her through such suffering again?

And yet, secretly, she wants him to ignore every word she says.

On their last day at the hotel before leaving for Shillong, Wallace comes out onto the veranda to find her asleep in a chair, her book fallen on the floor. Her hair is wispy on her neck, her breath causing the lace on her bodice to flutter, her face grey and crumpled. The sight fills him with pity. My wife, he thinks, for better and for worse.

Margaret wakes to the pressure of his mouth in her hair. His urgent, *Darling, don't ever leave me alone again* ... On the cusp between sleeping and waking, she cannot be sure if the words she is hearing are imagined or real. Dredging herself up into a state of such longing that it takes her breath away. Then she thinks, what if a servant came into the room? It wouldn't do to show such emotion in public.

As nerveless as a teacher calling a roll, she answers, 'Of course, Wallace, I won't leave you.'

'It is a boy.'

Wallace presses his face down on the desk. A boy. The smell of leather and wood in his nostrils. Dust in his eyes threatens tears. His heart thumping as if he has run uphill. *A boy* ... Momentarily he is lost. From adulterous passion, fornication, sinfulness and shame, a boy is born. The old pain lodges inside him. His dearest wish is to have him back: the infant mouldering in his grave. God's will be done, but to what purpose? God's word was not heeded: *A man who commits adultery has no sense: whoever does so destroys himself.* Well, he has no sense, that is indisputable. He is a foolish man who has defiled the memory of one dead son with the birth of another. A loathsome man. In the past, he prided himself as a person of virtue, of honesty and kindness. And now that man is no more, destroyed by his venality. In anguish, he beats his forehead on the mahogany desk.

'All is well,' Bon says, a smile hovering.

He lifts up his head. 'What?'

'Baia and baby are well.'

Wallace stands up, swaying angrily, wiping his cheeks with his fists. To have shown such emotion before a servant. Is there no end to his humiliation?

Through clenched teeth, he mutters, 'God must have a sense of humour.'

Bon is his only confidant. In his narrow circle of Shillong, exposure is a terrifying prospect. He can't tell any of the men he knows about his predicament. The club is a vortex of tittle-tattle circulated by wives who have too much time on their hands. Wallace is a practical man who prides himself on being able to find a solution to any problem. Bon becomes his trusted go-between. Through him, Wallace had made arrangements to provide Baia with money during her confinement. Now there is a baby to provide for as well.

That night he dreams he is riding through the forest, an infant strapped to his side. Above the treetops, a virgin moon casts its light onto a chasm below. His horse, whinnying with fear, pulls back from the edge. Wallace stands up in his saddle, unstraps the infant and lifts it high above his head.

He wakes up, squirming in the bed. Beside him, Margaret does not stir. He envies her ability to sleep as she does, guilt-free and ignorant. For a long time he stays awake. Somehow, the nightmare has unfettered his mind: he is thinking clearly at last. He knows what he has to do. Firstly, Margaret must never know the truth about Baia and the baby. He will salvage whatever remnants of propriety he has: he will choose deceit over decency. Kindness dictates that his honour be subject to a tawdry trade-off. So be it: he follows his conscience as best he can. Secondly, his wife and daughters will be cared for and protected. During the day, the house is so quiet without the girls, their busyness and chatter. How he misses them! Little Alexandra is being spoilt by his mother and sisters in Seacon. 'Alexa is the apple of my eye,' his mother writes in her last letter. But does she remember her daddy? He is afraid to ask. Thirdly, Margaret and he will travel to Ireland for a visit in the following year. He is due some leave then. Until now he's been worried about the complications of a trip home, the cost and the time it would take but he is determined that his family will come first. Margaret wants so much to see the girls and he is keen to know how the plans for the new house at Seacon are progressing. Fourthly, he decides, he will visit Baia. While his sense of duty has been sullied, it is still intact. He will go to see her, albeit in secret, to acknowledge his son.

When Wallace arrives, Baia's mother is so frightened at the sight of a white man she gets out of her sick bed and stumbles away. Baia didn't know that *mei* has such strength in her skinny little legs.

'Babu!' she shouts when he enters. Crouching under the eaves, he is too big and awkward. It is all too much for the little house: her Uncle Bon and him together crowding in to see the baby, wrapped in a cloth at her breast.

'Be careful,' she says as she hands him over, but Wallace is gentleness itself, cradling the baby who wriggles and laughs in his arms.

'His name is Hajom.'

A puzzled look. Then, 'Aye, of course. Mr Kissor Singh's name.'

Baia holds her breath, watching his thumb being gripped by tiny fingers and his head bent low to kiss the downy head, to examine the baby's feet.

'He looks like you, Baia.'

'But see how long he is! He will be a giant, just like his father.'

His father ...

He places the baby in her arms, turns and walks away.

XIV

IRELAND 1922

When Wallace and Margaret arrive in Dublin on a visit they spend a few days in the city before travelling to the school at Brookfield to see the girls. The youngest girl is by then old enough to join her two sisters. At the age of seven, Alexandra is tall and fair and hangs back shyly while Maggie and Elizabeth skitter around in excitement at the prospect of a trip on the train to Belfast to visit Aunt Molly and the cousins. The oldest girl, Maggie, has acquired a pair of spectacles that give her the air of a bluestocking, and Elizabeth is prettier than ever. The youngest girl has changed most of all.

'Lord, I wouldn't recognise you, Alexandra,' Wallace exclaims. 'How you have grown.'

'Daddy,' she says, gazing up at him. 'Everyone calls me Alexa now.'

And he is reminded of seeing her face for the first time. Her cold blue stare.

At Belfast station Wallace parts company with the others and travels on, by train, to Ballymoney. After all the chatter and fuss he is content to be alone. The girls are well – that is all he needs to know. On parting, Alexa even overcomes her shyness sufficiently to give him a timid embrace.

His brother James is waiting for him at the railway station in Ballymoney. He is dressed in a tweed suit and brown brogues, looking every inch a country doctor. At the architect's office, the man himself ushers them in to show them the drawings. As he spreads them out on the table, a smell of new ink tickles Wallace's nostrils.

'You can see there are three bedrooms and a small one for the maid.' The architect's pencil travels across the paper like a spider, moving aside one drawing to display another. 'Here is the kitchen, the dining room and the drawing room.'

James nudges him. 'A drawing room, no less.'

'Do you want me to go with you to see mam?' James asks.

'No, I'll talk to her,' Wallace says. 'The new house must be built.'

Otherwise, he will have failed, and his mother and sisters will be stuck in the damp old house with its rickety roof and smelly latrine. The construction of a fine new house will send out a message to everyone in Seacon that the McKay boys are doing well for themselves. Of course, James is making his contribution, but he, Wallace, is the oldest son. Steeling himself, he stands outside the old house and resolves to take no excuses. Then he goes inside to confront the peeling plaster, the cracked windows, the draught under the door, and finds his mother, wrapped in a mountain of shawls, sitting in her rocking chair up close to the range.

Without a word they embrace so tightly that he hears the sob in her throat.

'Too long away,' she murmurs, pushing him away. 'Too long away.'

He pats her shoulder. 'I'm here now.'

'Throw by that old hat,' she said, 'and sit yourself down.'

He does what he is told and gives her all the news about Margaret and the girls while his mother makes him a cup of tea. Once she is seated again, he doesn't waste any time, tells her about his meeting with the architect, and how the plans for the house exceed his expectations. She pulls the shawls around her and squints at the kettle.

'Do you hear me?' he says. 'The men will be here in a month's time to clear the site.'

'All that trouble,' she mutters, 'and the money!'

'This is for your own good,' he says loudly.

'I'm not deaf. There's no need to snap the head off me.'

'Mam,' he relents, 'there's nothing to be afraid of.'

It is an invitation for his mother to rear up. 'I'll have you know I'm afeard of nothing.'

He drums his fingers on his knees and waits as she rocks backwards and forwards. At last, she looks up at him and asks, 'Is it really what you want, son?'

'Aye, it is.'

'Man dear, since you want it so much, then I must oblige.'

It doesn't feel like a victory – more like capitulation. When he gets up to leave and bends over to kiss her cheek, her skin is paper-thin. Will she live long enough to see the house built? He closes his eyes and, for a moment, imagines the sheets of thick cartridge paper lifting like birds from the architect's desk.

On their way back to Dublin, having settled the girls in school, Wallace and Margaret spend a night in Lurgan. The hotel has an abandoned air as if it has seen better days. Is anyone there? they wonder as they wait on the step until an old man opens the door. Apart from themselves, no one else is sitting in the dining room. Dinner is a thin stew, followed by bowls of apple tart and custard. As soon as they finish their meal they go upstairs to a chilly, unwelcoming bedroom. Both are struck by the contrast with the hotel in Calcutta, the warm air whispering from the punka wallahs' fans, the elaborate copper chandeliers.

'Wouldn't be surprised if this place is haunted.' Wallace says as he switches off the light and slides between the clammy sheets.

'Wallace, you're freezing!'

'I won't be for long,' he says, nuzzling her neck. 'Lord, I'll be glad to get back to Shillong.'

'Aye,' she whispers, 'me too.'

They lie close together as the heat of their bodies works its magic. This is what he wants: the comfort of marriage, her breast cupped in his hand. He pictures a future in which they grow old together in the shelter of wedlock and respectability. Even as she sleeps, he is unable to banish the constant presence of a golden-skinned child created out of the Assam sun. The boy is four years old and growing tall. No matter how imperfect a father he might be, Wallace is determined that the child will have a good education, even if he doesn't know how. Then, out of nowhere, comes the answer.

Miss Barr.

Of course.

His yelp of glee wakes Margaret.

'It's alright, dear,' he belches, 'the stew has given me dyspepsia.'

'Wallace, manners!'

'Pardon me.'

When he is back in Shillong he will ask Miss Barr to take the boy into her school. Wallace trusts her. No matter what she thinks, Miss Barr will not judge him.

In the darkness, Margaret murmurs, 'wouldn't you think she'd be grateful?'

Wallace chooses not to defend his mother. He is tired and wants to sleep.

'The house will get built. That is what matters.'

'All that money,' she murmurs into her pillow.

'Now, Margaret, stop it.'

So forceful is his squeeze that, for once, she doesn't argue.

XV

'When I'm here, I dream of Dublin and when I'm home, I dream of India,' Margaret says to Wallace, 'Isn't that the limit?'

He is only half-listening. Now that they are back in Shillong and lodged inside the bungalow for the rainy season, it feels as if they have come to some unspoken agreement to be kind to each other. Outside the rain chatters in the drains. Indoors all is quiet. In the half-world of the monsoon he is at ease with his surroundings: the book shelves climbing to the ceiling, the fires burning in the grates. Margaret and he get up late and pass the day in a hazy rhythm of eating and reading. They often spend their evenings at the club. She is an energetic participant: a member of the races committee and the principal organiser of bridge parties and concerts. Anything, she says, to break the monotony. When he returns from tours of the tea gardens, it is a relief to be home. At Christmas there is a party at the club and people wear silly hats and play charades. On New Year's Eve they blow whistles when the clock in the dining hall strikes midnight. In spring they go on outings in the hills or have picnics at Wards Lake.

Wallace stands up from the breakfast table. 'I'm going to visit Miss Barr.'

Margaret looks up from her boiled egg. 'What, again?'

'Well, you know she needs help with her monthly accounts. The church in England want every penny to be accounted for. Anyway, it is time I was off, before you get fed up with me.'

'I sometimes think you see more of that woman, these days, than you do of me.'

'If that's true – and I don't believe it is, dearest – it's because you are so popular at the club that you have no time for me.'

She laughs. 'What nonsense!'

How smoothly, he thinks, the falsehoods flow.

'That reminds me. You will be back in time for the recital tonight, won't you? Lavinia will be cross otherwise.'

He groans inwardly. 'How could I forget? Will I ask Miss Barr to join us?'

'Oh yes, please do. It's going to be super, Lavinia says.'

'Then I wouldn't miss it for the world. I promise.'

Promise is a word that has no value. The marriage vow, the pledge of loyalty: my word is my bond. His word counts for nothing. Growing into the part of deceiver has been surprisingly easy. He will attend the recital with Margaret because it is something he can do for her. Everything else is a lie. There are times he stands outside himself as if to assess how closely he mines his secret latitude, where he moves freely about and which Margaret will never penetrate. It is a source of amazement to him that she does not detect the charlatan in him. She is a clever woman and yet foolish enough to have become, unwittingly, a creature of convenience in his life.

Miss Barr's school is located in a part of the town of Shillong not frequented by Europeans. It consists of one room made of wood and bamboo and has a corrugated iron roof. In the rainy season, the roof leaks and the street outside is a sea of mud. The young children sit on the floor and learn their lessons by rote. They are taught to read and write but, unlike in the mission schools elsewhere in Shillong, they are not given religious instruction.

'I am here to educate these children. I've no intention of filling their heads with doctrine. I tell them all the world's religions are the same,' Miss Barr says.

Wallace listens without comment.

'I do hope that, one day, my dream will come true.' Miss Barr has made clear to him that her ambition is to return to the hills as soon as she can to open a school there. 'In the meantime, Mr McKay, I'm required to stay in Shillong, but I will go back to where I'm needed most.'

Each time he comes to the little school, Wallace marvels at Miss Barr's courage. He admires strong women, he married Margaret after all. He likes their certainty, their forthrightness, their lack of guile. When he makes his confession to her, Miss Barr does not disappoint him. She hears him out and, without comment, proposes that Baia come and stay at the school. She can help me, she said. I will make a teacher out of her.

'And Hajom?'

'He is a little young but I will take him anyway.'

Wallace's mind is in turmoil. He is indebted to her. How can he ever thank her?

He says, 'I am so sorry to burden you with my responsibilities.'

'There are worse sins. Between life and death, which do you think is more desirable?'

He looks at her, puzzled.

'What I mean to say is that you haven't killed anyone, have you?'

He laughs, despite himself.

Now, among the children, the boy sits cross-legged on a mat in the schoolroom, chanting his lessons. Hajom is a beautiful child, with the black hair and yellow-gold skin of a Khasi. When he looks up he sees the tall white man who says he is his father. The boy's eyes resemble those of his Irish grandmother. Every time Wallace visits Hajom, he is met by the pale-blue gaze of Eliza McKay. Their conversation is stilted and, invariably, short. The man's shyness renders him inarticulate, while the boy is in awe of the stranger from whom, his mother tells him, all munificence comes. It is a relief when Miss Barr comes in to ask Wallace to examine the school accounts and the boy is free to run home through the streets to tell his mother about the man who had given him ruppees and called him *khun*.

'Margaret hopes you will come to the club tonight for a recital.'

'How kind of her!' Miss Barr beams. 'Yes, I'd be happy to join you both. Maybe I'll meet someone in the know who can help me get my new school.'

He is aware of the struggle Miss Barr has to convince the church authorities of the merits of her work.

'You know I will always help you.'

'Oh, Mr McKay, you are a dear friend but what I need is an officious official with a satchel full of papers and a fountain pen in his pocket.'

After the recital has come to a close, the musicians strike up *God Save the King* and the audience push back their chairs with a clatter.

'Oh, for heaven's sake,' Margaret groans as she hauls herself up, 'not this malarkey again. What are we asking God to save the King *from*, exactly?'

Miss Barr murmurs, 'Retribution, do you think?'

And Margaret giggles.

After the singing is done, the three of them follow the crowd into the dining room where drinks are being served. They sit down at a low table and, for a moment, no one speaks. Miss Barr gazes around at the crowd of government officials, professional men, tea planters and their wives.

'Not a brown face among them,' she says. 'It is how imperialism crushes this land like the insatiable monster it is.'

Margaret is astonished. 'Do you really believe it could be any different?'

'I most certainly do.'

Margaret shakes her head. 'The people here aren't able to govern themselves. They are too feckless.'

'Oh, really?' Miss Barr looks interested. 'Just like the Irish, do you mean?'

'I *beg* your pardon?'

'Don't you see? Your country has shown the way. Oh, Mrs McKay, aren't you proud of what Ireland has accomplished?'

'It's different here,' Margaret exclaims. 'I mean to say.'

'To win independence for your country is a remarkable achievement. It is a lesson not lost here in India, I can tell you.'

Margaret looks unconvinced.

Miss Barr continues. 'The independence of India will follow. It is only a matter of time, believe me. I've attended meetings. I've even lectured on the subject, and already I can see there is a change in the way people think. It is palpable, even among Indian women.'

Wisely Wallace doesn't join in their conversation. He is in the company of the two people who know him best, albeit each in their own way, and he treads carefully. Politics doesn't interest him. He likes to know how the physical world is constructed: the different forms in nature, how man's ingenuity can shape them for the better. He withdraws into his own thoughts. The book he intends to write isn't turning out as he had planned. On his travels around Assam, he has taken photographs and written copious notes but the information gathered is far from exhaustive. Across the dining room, he recognises a tea planter he hasn't seen for years, a man well-equipped to expand his knowledge of pests and diseases in the cultivation of tea.

'Excuse me ladies. Just going to have a word.'

The women are too engrossed in conversation to notice. Relieved, Wallace makes his escape.

Miss Barr takes a sip from her glass of tonic water. 'Will you be staying much longer, Mrs McKay?'

'For goodness sake, please call me Margaret.'

'Ah, of course, you are Margaret, just like I am. The Khasis can't pronounce my name so they call me Kong Barr.'

Kong Barr, a suitably plain name Margaret thinks for a plain-speaking woman, who makes such an interesting companion with her homespun frock and sensible shoes.

'Oh, I expect we'll be leaving soon. Wallace likes an early night.'

Miss Barr smiles, 'I mean will you be staying much longer in Shillong? I suppose I have a vested interest. Wallace has become my accountant by default. He has helped me out of many a muddle, I can tell you.'

Margaret feels a spark of resentment. Wallace is my husband, she wants to point out, but she is slightly in awe of Miss Barr.

'It is time we went home to Ireland,' she says, 'I have daughters in school there.'

The understanding is that Wallace and she will make their home in Dublin eventually, but they have never settled on when exactly they will leave. Now the prospect crystallizes into an imperative.

'Wallace's contract is up in less than a year's time,' she says. 'We will go home then.'

She knows she should discuss the matter with Wallace before confiding in Miss Barr, but what difference does it make? If she doesn't make a stand, Wallace would quite happily stay in India forever. Being in the other woman's company unsettles Margaret as much as it intrigues her. Their lives are poles apart: here is a woman alone and pursuing her ambition in the most difficult of circumstances. Margaret admires such singularity of purpose. She finds it an inspiration. Her mind is made up: she has sacrificed enough.

'Yes,' she says again. 'We will go home then.'

XVI

For the occasion, Margaret puts on her best hat. She carries an armful of flowers in from the garden and arranges them in a basket, white flowers for innocence. Secreted in the basket is a small teddy bear. Not wishing to be thought sentimental, she does not mention it to anyone. She found it under a chest of drawers when everything in the house was being packed up and ready for transporting. The teddy bear is battered and has lost an eye but the girls were fond of the old thing.

'Saying goodbye is difficult,' she tells Wallace. 'I prefer to go there on my own.'

How could he understand how she feels? They were the worst days of her life: her baby struggled so valiantly and she could not save him. No man could understand.

This is the last time Margaret will climb the steps into the cemetery, the last time to follow the path between the headstones, to arrive at the grave with the proper headstone she insisted upon. The last time to bring flowers to her baby's grave. There is no one about: she is completely alone. She kneels down and places the flowers on the grave, then removes her gloves, and with her bare hands, digs a hole in the earth. When the hole is big enough, she puts the teddy bear into it and covers it over.

'Teddy will keep you safe,' she whispers.

No one will guess the grave has been disturbed. Even if they do, they won't know why. She would like to pray, but any prayers she knows seem worthless: strings of words, designed to keep death at bay. Maybe a hymn would do instead, a lullaby for the child. Uncertainly, she begins to sing and the words come, such sweet words that she fights the urge to weep. Strewn on the grave, the flowers exude a faint perfume. They won't last long, another day at most, she thinks. Death comes quickly in Shillong.

Meanwhile Wallace is saying his own goodbyes. He has arranged to meet Baia and Miss Barr after the school is finished for the day. He arrives, carrying his camera, to find the two women sitting down, side by side, in Miss Barr's cramped sitting room. Miss Barr pours tea and they make stilted conversation until Wallace can't bear it any longer. He stands up, coughs, bows slightly to the women and begins. He wants to make clear to them both that he will continue, come what may, to pay for the boy's education. For Hajom's education, he corrects himself. The women smile at each other, as if there were any doubt. He outlines how the payments will be made through a solicitor and how he wishes to support Miss Barr too, in her efforts to build her new school by giving a modest financial contribution whenever the time comes. When he is finished he sits down. For a moment the only sounds are of hawkers calling in the street outside.

'Another cup?' Miss Barr offers to fill Wallace's teacup. He frowns at the floor, looking miserable.

She takes pity on him. 'You're such a good friend; you have never let us down.' She replaces the teapot on its stand. 'We will have to manage without you from now on. Isn't that right, Baia?'

'Hajom is my life,' Baia says quietly. 'I want only the best for him.'

'And he will have the best, I promise,' Miss Barr says. 'He's a bright boy. Studies hard at school and is quick to learn. He could make it all the way to university. What do you think, Wallace?'

For a moment he stares at her. Then he starts to laugh. The sound of his laughter is too loud for the little sitting room but the women, relieved at the change in his mood, laugh with him.

'There is nothing I'd like more than to have my son go all the way.'

'I don't understand,' Baia says in alarm. She looks fearfully, first at Wallace and then at Miss Barr. 'I don't want Hajom to go away.'

'We could try for Oxford,' Wallace says.

'Even better,' Miss Barr chuckles. 'Why not my old alma mater, Cambridge?'

They are too absorbed in their conversation to pay Baia any heed. She bows her head. She doesn't know what to say: they are making no sense.

At last Wallace remembers the camera. He stands up. 'It's time we went outside. I want a photograph, for the day that's in it.'

The two women follow him out into Miss Barr's little garden. The light is better outdoors, he says, glad to see that the boy is waiting, his hair combed, his shirt and trousers clean and white.

'Miss Barr, will you do the honours please?' Wallace offers her the camera. 'Look, that's the button you press. Now, Baia and Hajom, you must stay absolutely still while Miss Barr takes our photograph.'

Baia stands beside her son and he stands on Hajom's other side. Without thinking, he puts his arm around the boy's shoulders. Despite the afternoon heat, Wallace feels ice in the air.

Time is running out ...

'You are all looking far too solemn!' Miss Barr cries. Their smiles freeze as the shutter opens and closes. Frozen for all time, Wallace thinks. To his consternation, he feels his arm trembling on Hajom's shoulder. In the next instant, every part of his body is shaking. The realisation overwhelms him that he is about to lose forever, the fine, mysterious boy who belongs half in Wallace's world, half in another. He is unable to speak. The prospect of parting with Hajom is unbearable.

For a moment they stand without moving.

'Come on, Baia,' Miss Barr says. 'Let us go inside.'

Wallace's heart lightens when he sees the boy does not follow the women into the house.

'Well, Hajom ...'

He wants to pull the boy close to him: to feel the thatch of dark hair on his cheek, to whisper messages that only Hajom will hear and remember all his life. What the words might be, Wallace does not know. For a long moment he struggles to speak. He is conscious of the women watching through the window. It is hopeless. Filled with despair, he shakes hands with his son.

'Always be a good boy,' he says, 'and look after your mother.'

By coincidence, both Margaret and Wallace arrive back at the bungalow at the same time. He opens the gate and Margaret walks on ahead.

'Oh, Wallace,' she says. 'I feel so much better now. You have no idea.'

She is so absorbed in describing her visit to the cemetery, that she doesn't ask him how he has spent his day, for which he is grateful. He clears his throat, tears pricking his eyes.

'Darling,' Margaret says, touched by his emotion, 'we must remember that our little boy is in heaven.'

Not trusting himself to speak, he trudges up the driveway after his wife. The ache inside his skull will lessen eventually. In the meantime, he must find a way to remember everything about the boy dressed in white, who waited for him in an Indian garden. He will not forget the warmth of the boy's hand in his. Wallace McKay, he tells himself, you have a son, a beautiful boy; not that bundle of bones buried in the earth, with only a teddy bear for company.

XVII

The newspapers have been full of political upheaval: Irish waging war against British, then setting about to wage war against one another. There are times Margaret can't believe what she is reading: can scarcely hope that out of the upheaval a phoenix has risen: that the dream of national independence has come true. They are travelling home to Ireland for the last time and she tells anyone who will listen. 'When we left for India, we lived under British rule. Today we are going home to live in a Free State.'

Now that she is back in Dublin she wonders what does she expect? A transcendence in the air, excitement in the streets: some indefinable alteration to everything she has known. She has yearned for freedom in Ireland for so long. Now she wants to see it, taste it, smell it. To her dismay, the city looks worn out and decrepit, exhausted after its violent convulsions. The noise made by trams and motor cars are the sounds of commerce, not revolution. Deflated, Margaret walks past Trinity College and sees, to her disgust, a faded Union Jack hanging from a window.

As she approaches O'Connell Bridge, her mood lifts. Adorned with bunting and flowers, an elaborate, white and green painted pavilion dominates the thoroughfare. It could be a remnant of imperial glory, but it is not. It is the expression of a new Ireland: Irish Civic Week, a celebration of the new State. The day before, Wallace and she had stood in the rain and watched the pageant of industry pass the pavilion: a mile-long line of trucks and motor cars emblazoned with signs: *S. Varian & Co. Brushes; Carlow Sugar; the Municipal Technical School.* A stream of ladies dressed as Celtic goddesses had followed the vehicles. Little tin crowns tilted on their foreheads gave them an air of intoxication. The parade was a such an utilitarian affair Margaret did not know what to make of it. Its plainness appealed to her, but it is not the kind of parade she is accustomed to. No thrilling sounds of bands playing, no military banners, no clashing cymbals. Over the years, her hackles have been raised by too many imperial displays.

She is reminded of her conversation with Mrs Caldwell on board ship all those years ago. The silly woman was delirious with delight, describing the pavilion erected in Delhi for the coronation of the Emperor of India. Such a marvellous sight, she said, although Mrs Caldwell hadn't even been in Delhi. Everything the woman knew about the coronation was hearsay. That hadn't stopped her burbling on. At her insistence, Margaret was expected to visualise the whole spectacle. On silk-swathed elephants, haughty, bejewelled Indian princes were forced to humiliate themselves before the emperor, plump George V, sitting on his throne, the imperial crown of diamonds, rubies, sapphires and emeralds perched on his head. Such stuff and nonsense. Margaret was glad she had made a stand, even if Mrs Caldwell refused to speak to her afterwards, and the two women spent the rest of the sea voyage avoiding each other.

And now, she thinks, how dreary everything looks. The pavilion will be dismantled and broken up in some corporation depot, its bright colours replaced by dingy quayside buildings looming out of the fog.

A gust of wind distracts her. She looks up at a tricolour fixed to a flagpole on the pavilion roof. The flag flaps noisily, reminding her of something.

What is it?

Then she remembers: in Shillong, that evening of the recital in the club, Miss Barr asked, 'Aren't you proud of what Ireland has accomplished?'

Margaret wishes that she had said then what she knows now.

Yes, I am proud.

There are times when the house in St Kevin's Park is like a railway station, with the girls racketting around and banging doors. She has to shout to make herself heard. Her daughters are now young women. So what does that make her? The question broods. She brushes it aside. The three girls are her prize, her future: Maggie, bespectacled and serious. Elizabeth, lovely enough to break men's hearts, and Alexa playing the piano like a crazed angel. The thought of the future is exhilarating; Margaret is confident her daughters will make something of themselves. Their world is so different to the one she has known: a new beginning in a changed Ireland.

She particularly enjoys Sundays when they are all together, in their best clothes, and heading to the Unitarian church on St Stephen's Green. The girls, giddy as show ponies, as they run towards the tram stop.

'Behave yourselves,' she says and, when they go quiet, she is sorry. Now that Wallace is doing a stint in the company's offices in London, the household is less tied to a routine. The cats sleep on the beds and the lights are left on all day, and when the butter knife goes missing she doesn't bother replacing it, so everyone digs their knives in the butter dish. Really, she should make more of an effort, but it is so pleasant to while away her time at bridge parties or reading books while the girls are at school.

One cold November Sunday, the four of them are walking up the steps of the church when she is distracted by a glimpse of white lace.

'Elizabeth!'

Surprised, her daughter turns to her.

'Your petticoat is showing.'

The girl's face turns crimson.

Margaret takes a pin from her hair and uses it to make a hasty adjustment.

'Are you sure it won't show?' Elizabeth cranes her neck to see the result.

'It will have to do.'

'But are you sure?'

Heavens, it's only a petticoat, Margaret wants to say but she is silent. There is no point in giving bad example.

The sound of organ music spills out to greet them as they arrive at the open doors. Such a doleful, wheezy sound. Of course, today is Armistice Day Remembrance Sunday. Many in the congregation are dressed in black, some women wear mourning veils. Margaret pities each one of them, although she has her suspicions about how many of them actually lost someone in the war. After all, there are only seven names on the memorial plaque on the wall. Family names she recognises. Two brothers. Young men led like lambs to the slaughter. She is wary of military displays of any kind. The empire should be a matter of shame, she feels, not veneration. *We fail to see the value of, or necessity for, blood sacrifice to reconcile God to man*, the Unitarian minister has preached on more than one occasion. She takes his meaning to heart. Today, out of respect for the dead, she will hold her tongue. This church is her spiritual home, the people here are as modest, thoughtful and resolutely intelligent as she aspires to be.

Margaret sees a familiar face in the congregation. Heavens, after all these years, Mrs Seymour is still with us, bent double and wearing that dreadful hat. Probably the same one she wore when her husband introduced her to Wallace for the first time. As frayed and moth-eaten as ever. Mr Seymour, no doubt, is long gone to his reward. The male of the species unable to last the pace. How queer to think that old Mrs Seymour is still grinding away here on Earth while the graves of France are stuffed full of the bodies of young men.

Margaret glances along the pew. The three girls are sitting demurely, hands on their laps, their hymnals before them. The loss of a child in any circumstance, she wants to confide in them, must be honoured, but there is no time, for the minister has already climbed into the pulpit. The service begins. She resolves to be quiet and good and give herself over to the service of remembrance. Her baby son lying on a hillside in Assam. We suffer in their coming and in their going. Who said that? Ah yes, that poor Mr Pearse, putting words in his mother's mouth. Margaret bends her head as the readings and hymns follow in melancholy waves. A mood of resignation fills the church. *Thy Will be done* ... Dinner will be ready by the time they get home. Did she tell the maid to baste the lamb? Lavinia Frobisher said she stopped going to church because, instead of praying, all she could ever think about was the bills she owed.

Suddenly the man seated beside Margaret lets out a deep sigh. At the sound of the organ, he stands up, swaying back on his heels. She waits while the music gathers strength. Around them the congregation bustles to its feet and then the voices burst out in unison, singing *God Save our Gracious King.*

Margaret stiffens. Her mind is on fire, her face is burning. The old empire is dead. A new republic is about to be born. For a moment she is speechless with rage.

'This is an outrage,' she cries out. 'I will not stand for it.'

Her protest, loud and brittle, rises above the other voices. A sense of her own power courses through her body. *Look at me.* She is encouraged by the shock on the faces turning towards the respectably dressed, red-faced lady stabbing the air with her folded umbrella. Alongside her, the three girls cringe. 'Mummy ...' Alexa, tugs at her mother's sleeve but Margaret is too maddened to notice. Sweeping her purse under her elbow, she pushes her way past the man beside her. Once she is standing in the centre aisle, she gives an imperious wave of her umbrella.

'Come along, girls,' she orders. 'We are leaving.'

Puce with embarrassment, the three girls follow their mother. As they pass, heads in the congregation swivel, the singing falters. The organist, a mild-mannered music teacher from the Academy, plays on, oblivious of the disturbance. Alarmed, the girls watch as their mother veers off towards him. When Margaret reaches the organist she shakes her fist.

'Long to reign over us?' she hisses loudly. 'Well, *fat chance* is what I say.'

The music expires in a stunned silence. The organist rocks back on his stool. Triumphantly, Margaret heads for the door, ushers the girls outside and lets the door slam behind her.

In the street, the girls move closer to one another, disconcerted by a sudden rush of air blowing leaves around them, and the sight of their mother, full of nervous energy and sparking with fury.

'The next time I see that minister, I'll give him a piece of my mind,' she says.

Maggie looks owlish. Alexa smothers her giggles. Elizabeth examines the sky. 'Shouldn't we go, Mummy?' she says. 'It's about to rain, I think.'

Margaret opens her umbrella and gives it a shake. Ignoring her daughters, she walks off down the street so quickly the girls have to hurry after her. At the corner of St Stephen's Green, Elizabeth stops and swings around to check her hem.

'Is my petticoat showing?' she wonders aloud, but no one is listening.

When their father returns from London, he brings presents and the girls make a fuss over him. Gradually, the mood in the house reverts: there is a calm in the rooms, the marshalling of the old order. Living in an all-female household, Margaret realises, has its drawbacks. Wallace's homecoming challenges her in a way that suits her. She likes the warmth of his arm draped along the back of her chair, his courteous ways. Even when they disagree, he is respectful, unlike some men she knows who treat their wives abominably, although when Margaret tells him over breakfast about the blow she struck against the British empire, he honks with laughter.

'It's nothing to laugh about.'

'Darling,' he is apologetic. 'But remembering the war dead is hardly a crime.'

'As a good Protestant I must protest. Our church being used as a bastion of reaction, it doesn't bear thinking about.'

Thoughtfully, Wallace chews on a slice of toast.

'Tolerance is a virtue,' he says. 'Can't we just live and let live?'

'No,' she bristles. 'Else we will never escape the pernicious influence of empire.'

He hides his face in his newspaper and gives a vague *if you say so, dear.*

'It's easy for you. I have to hold the fort here while you're off gallivanting.'

The newspaper drops. An eyebrow is raised. Gallivanting?

'I'm sorry,' she says, chastened. 'I didn't mean to be rude.'

His look is contemplative, his eyes hooded. How handsome he is.

'I am so glad you're home.'

His face breaks open in a smile. 'I'm glad to be home too. I miss you when I'm away.'

'Oh, Wallace, even when I'm rude?'

'My dear, you can be rude sometimes.' To her astonishment he blows her a kiss. 'But, believe me, you are *never* dull.'

'I think that's the nicest thing you've ever said to me.'

He guffaws. 'Touché.'

Eager to make amends she stands up. 'I'll put away your things. I can't trust the maid to do it properly.'

Wallace folds up the newspaper. 'By the way, I'll be gone all day. The allotments are ready. At last, the unemployed can learn the art of growing vegetables, whether they want to or not.'

He is an enthusiastic member of a charitable club that provides practical education to the poor of Dublin. 'Keeps me busy when I'm home,' he often says. 'Otherwise, I'd go mad.'

Now that Wallace is home, maybe they will go to the theatre or make a trip to the Zoological Gardens. Soon it will be Christmas and the whole family will be together for the first time in years. She lingers for a moment on the landing and imagines Wallace, standing out in a ploughed field, tall, hatless, gesticulating as he addresses a group of men in shirtsleeves leaning on their spades. All in all, she has as good a husband as a man can be.

The trunk stands in the middle of the bedroom floor. Her job is to empty it. Any dirty clothing goes into the laundry basket. Anything unused is folded and put into the wardrobe. The books are set aside for his office. Boots and shoes laid out to be polished. As she has done many times before, Margaret unwraps her husband's life and puts it back together again in an act of intimacy. Of love even. In her nostrils, a mixture of smells: sweat, dampness, dirt, as she bundles shirts and under-linen into the laundry basket. At the bottom of the trunk is Wallace's brown work coat. She lifts it out and presses it to her face. The old cotton coat smells of tea. It reminds her of India: the whiff of magnolia in the air, warm evenings on the veranda, the sound of mynah birds screeching in the trees. In the far reaches of Assam they were companions at arms. Now she stays at home while Wallace is poised to keep on travelling. The Company want him to go to Africa next, he told her as soon as he arrived back from London. Kenya. To assess its potential for growing tea. Listening to him, she felt a flash of envy. What if she shed her responsibilities and ran away to the jungle with him? Is at his side while he carves out a tea garden in the wilderness? Vivid in her mind are the rows of small-leaved shrubs shaded by acacias. She feels the twigs brush against her skirt. No, tea isn't a shrub, she recalls. Tea is a tree.

Against her cheek she feels something, stiff and crackling, in the folds of Wallace's work coat. Whatever it is she must remove it for safekeeping. It could be ruined in the laundry, otherwise. She spreads the coat on the bed and searches through the pockets. Nothing to be found. Puzzled, she begins to bundle up the coat again and is about to throw it in the basket when she sees an inside breast pocket that she hasn't noticed before.

It comes out easily: a piece of paper with tattered edges that she turns over in her hand. A photograph, about three inches high, three inches broad with a scalloped margin all around it.

Just a photograph, is her first thought.

Three faces gaze back at her. The man towers over the other two, a lugubrious expression on his face. The woman, tiny, round-faced, is familiar. Margaret would know her anywhere. Between the man and the woman stands a boy. A boy dressed all in white. He is taller than the woman. Margaret stares at the boy's mop of black hair, his round, smiling face and knows instantly that Baia is his mother.

A photograph that Wallace keeps close to his heart is her second thought.

She knows, then, by the way her husband's arm encircles the boy's shoulder, that he is the boy's father. She cannot breathe, her ribs tightening in her chest as the bedroom walls cave in.

In Grafton Street, nobody notices her white-faced anguish. To her relief, nobody cares. Somehow it is important to be with other people, and she welcomes the swirl of the crowds. She is comforted by the broken laughter, the rattle and thud of passing motorcars. Once she was secure, blithely so. Now there is nothing to hold on to. At the door of the Catholic church, a woman sits with a baby bundled up tight on her shoulder. Margaret rummages in her purse and drops coins into the outstretched hand. Another time she would have passed by the woman, but everything has changed: Margaret has become party to the world's suffering now. A man in a tattered jacket is chanting prayers before a statue of the Sacred Heart. He rocks back and forth like a toy clown.

Even if she wanted to, Margaret cannot pray.

She goes through the glass doors of Switzers & Co and plunges into its glowing interior of brass and polished wood. In the linen department upstairs she buys a set of sheets and pillowcases and waits for the counter girl to parcel them up in brown paper and string. His dirty linen. Her clean linen. She will exchange one for the other.

The house is quiet when she comes in. There is only the maid in the kitchen, who doesn't hear her turn the key in the lock. Margaret creeps upstairs to the bedroom and sets about stripping the bed, chucking the used sheets into the laundry basket. The new bed linen is full of promise, billowing out over the mattress like the sail of a boat. She tucks in the sheets, then slips the pillows into their new coverings. Only the bedspread defeats her: so big and awkward that she ends up on the floor, floundering in a mass of eiderdown. Suddenly exhausted, she leans her head against the bed, closes her eyes and finds herself rocking like the old man outside the church, and wailing like a lost child. In the past she tried to imagine how she would feel if Wallace died before she did. Now she knows the truth: there is no Wallace. The man she married never existed. There is someone else occupying his skin: a stranger whose life is full of betrayal.

Perhaps it is her fault, perhaps she deserves this agony. Has she been a bad wife – too cold, too unkind, the cause of her husband's adultery? She can't bear to think about that. All she knows is that her life is a lie and that she is drowning in a sea of pain. She whispers to herself, over and over, forbidden words, too frightening to be said. At last, she dries her tears on her sleeve and says aloud, *I am alone*. She holds her breath, but the flood of terror does not sweep her into oblivion. I am alone, she says again to her ravaged reflection in the mirror.

'And what,' her reflection wants to know, 'do you intend to do about it?'

'Are you ill, Mummy?'

How long has she been asleep? Margaret struggles up, groggy, to find Maggie standing at her bedside. Long shadows extend across the room. It is afternoon and the girls are home from school. She stares down at the torn fragments of the photograph scattered on the floor.

'Mummy?'

Margaret sinks back into the pillow. Her tongue feels thick and dry. She mutters, 'I'm alright, it's just my time of the month.'

'Are you sure?'

'Yes,' her tone is sharper than she intended. 'I am certain, yes.'

In the darkening room she can think only of escape. Nothing else matters. I will not spend another night under this roof, she tells her reflection in the mirror. It's a relief to know what to do. She takes her suitcase out of the wardrobe. As she packs, she feels almost light-hearted as if, for a moment, she has forgotten her reason for leaving. It is evening by the time she comes into the dining room, wearing her hat and coat and carrying the suitcase.

Seated around the table, with an assortment of textbooks at their elbows, the girls look up from their homework.

'Tell your father I'm taking the evening train,' Margaret says. 'I'm going to visit Alice Poots.'

The girls stare at her in amazement. Maggie's pen falls onto her open exercise book, splattering ink, but she is too distracted to notice.

'To Belfast, at this hour?'

'*Why* are you going?'

'What about us?'

Alexa's lower lip quivers. The youngest child, how sheltered she is, her mother thinks. I must not be undermined.

'No more questions, girls,' she says. 'I'll be back in a few days. Daddy will be in charge and Martha will mind you.'

Maggie stands up, her spectacles flashing. 'But she's only the maid.'

Margaret retorts, 'And I am only your mother.'

The cowed room waits.

'Now, all of you,' her tone softens, 'give me a kiss.'

The girls jostle around her like sheep in a pen. Their cheeks are warm on hers. A small hand strokes the fur collar of her coat. When Alexa steps away she is calm.

'Please, Mummy,' she says, 'will you bring us back presents?'

XVIII

This new border is an abomination, Margaret thinks as the train travels into Northern Ireland. With an imperial stroke of the pen, Ireland has been broken in two. It won't be long, she is convinced, until Ireland is united as a republic at last. Later that night, over tea and toast by the fireside, she shares this thought with her friend Alice, who looks at her in horror.

'Over my dead body,' her friend says. 'No Rome Rule for me, thank you very much.'

When Alice Poots opened her front door, the last person she expected to see is Margaret, wet and bedraggled on the doorstep, clutching a suitcase and an umbrella blown inside out by the wind.

'Come in, come in,' she ushers her in to sit by the fire. Did she get a chill on her way from the railway station? Poor thing, what on earth got into her, to be so far from home on a stormy night?

A sudden wave of anger threatens Margaret.

'I'm sorry. I'm a nuisance,' she says. 'I could stay in lodgings.'

Alice, the soul of kindness, insists, 'I won't hear another word, my dear. You must stay, you look terrible. Now take off your coat and I'll make you a nice cup of tea.'

There are cats everywhere: two tabbies, a small black and white, and a dirty grey. With a cry, Alice shoos the tabbies off the armchair to make room for the visitor. Secretly she is thankful there are fresh sheets on the bed in the spare room. She will pop a hot water bottle in the bed while Margaret is drying out by the fire. Her friend looks so poorly: red-eyed, tendrils of hair streeling down onto her collar. How sad to see that Margaret McKay has lost her looks. She was a bonny young woman once.

'Buck up, you'll feel better after a night's sleep,' she says. 'Tomorrow we'll have a nice long chat.'

Next morning Margaret tells Alice everything. Behind her dignified exterior anger seethes, but she is determined not to show any emotion. As the story unfolds, Alice is aghast.

'With a darkie! Oh, dear Lord, how could he?'

Margaret doesn't answer.

'Are you sure?'

'Oh yes,' Margaret's voice is gelid. 'I am absolutely sure.'

A tear glints in Alice's eye.

Margaret grimaces. 'You must promise me that anything I have said will not travel outside of this room.'

'Not even to your sister?'

'I definitely don't want Molly to know. She'd have it around the family in no time. I'll tell her myself in time.'

Alice dabs her eyes with her handkerchief. 'What about the girls?'

'Of course they don't know.'

'I mean where are they?'

'I left them in Dublin with Wallace.'

Alice looks down and absentmindedly strokes the cat on her lap. When she lifts her head Margaret can see fear in her eyes.

'My dear, do you think that was wise?'

Margaret shrugs.

'I mean, think what happened to poor Mrs McCann.'

'I don't understand.'

'Oh golly, I keep forgetting you were out foreign for so long. Her husband sold all their furniture and locked her out of the house. Then he took the children and disappeared down south.'

'I haven't the faintest idea what you're talking about.'

'You *must* remember. Mrs McCann was a Presbyterian married to a Roman Catholic and they had two children and were perfectly happy until a priest informed Mr McCann that they weren't married at all. They were living in sin according to that new Popish decree they brought in, *Ne Temere*.

'I don't see.'

'It was terrible. Mrs McCann refused to be married in a Roman Catholic church.'

'Well, good for her.'

'Oh no!' Alice cries. 'The poor woman was never right after.' Tears trickle down her plump cheeks. 'All her life she kept searching but she never saw her two weans ever again.'

'I don't see what that has to do with me.'

'Don't you see? In Westminster, your beloved Home Rule MPs backed Mr McCann up to the hilt. The Free State, my eye. There is no freedom to be had for Protestant people down south. We're having our own Stormont parliament now, thank the Lord.'

'When did this happen, Alice?'

'Oh, years and years ago.'

Alice is a dear friend, Margaret thinks, but when it comes to politics, she was always a bit of a fool. Wallace McKay would never be so cruel as to use the children against her.

Then she thinks: how do I know what he might do?

She is suddenly fearful. 'Oh, Alice.'

Her friend grasps Margaret's hands. 'Let me ask the Reverend Parks. He'll know what's best.'

'I don't think anyone can help me.'

It is hopeless. She came to Belfast in the expectation that her friend, the girls and she could set up house together. Alice could do with some company now, rattling around the big house since her husband died. Two women and three girls all together: it is Margaret's idea of independence. Sitting in Alice's feline-filled parlour, however, she sees it for what it is: a hare-brained scheme hatched in a moment of temporary insanity.

'Let me try, anyway,' Alice says and Margaret is too dejected to protest.

The following day, Alice sits in her kitchen, with one eye on the clock, while the Unitarian minister and Margaret sit in the parlour and talk. How long does it take, Alice wonders, to convince a woman where her duty lies? She has enough to be doing without all this commotion. Margaret coming here is all very well but Alice dreads the possibility of her staying indefinitely. After Jimmy, her husband, died Alice was bereft for a while but she isn't one to live in the past. To her surprise, she has come to enjoy her widowhood and, despite what people say, she is never lonely, for the dear cats are enough company for any woman. To her relief when the minister and Margaret re-appear it is obvious that the he has done the trick. Margaret is smiling, albeit wanly. The Unitarian minister is a long-chinned young man with a skeletal grin. 'Remember, it is within you ...' he murmurs to Margaret as he shakes her hand on leaving.

'What did he say?' Alice asks after the minister has gone.

'Is that kettle boiled?'

'What did he say, Margaret?'

'Oh, he told me to pull myself together and to think of the children.'

Margaret keeps the minister's words to herself, savouring her newfound strength: *'The stress and strain of life are great. The need for sane and balanced thought, and for mind and nerves under control is all the greater. The Kingdom of Heaven on Earth comes not by observation – not by decree or acts of Parliament, not by the compulsion of the tyrant, nor the ravings of the dogmatists. It must rise in millions of human hearts: it is within you.'*

Until now, her duty was clear: to teach her daughters right from wrong, to nurture their talents and encourage them in their studies. From now on, she has a new purpose: to ensure that their thoughts are sane and balanced and their minds and nerves are under control, so they can withstand any misfortune that life might throw at them.

Having said goodbye to a tearfully relieved Alice, Margaret travels back to Dublin on the train. She stares out of the window as the streets of red-brick terraces give away to rolling fields. How grateful she is that the minister did not mention forgiveness. Of one thing she is certain: she will never, ever forgive Wallace McKay.

XIX

Here it is, Wallace thinks, everything is out in the open at last. After the years of living with his lies and deceit, she is entitled to know the truth. To his surprise it is a relief to have been found out. To be given a chance to wipe the slate clean. And yet, the thought that Margaret may have left him for good fills him with such horror that when he hears her voice on the telephone, he can barely speak. All he can do is sit down at his desk and write her a letter.

> My dearest Margaret, I have done you a great wrong. I apologise with all my heart. You deserve better. You are upright and good while I am weak and culpable. I cannot excuse what I've done, yet here I am, asking you to forgive me. It would be easy to say that, in India, I was lonely without you and the girls. It's true: I was very lonely and missed you terribly. Easy to say too, that, in your absence, I lost all reason. That does not excuse my actions. The truth is that Baia made me alive in a way that I've never felt before. She is a poor servant girl who is entitled to your pity rather than your blame. The blame is mine. The child is mine. He is called Hajom. Please do not think I have forgotten how you suffered when our baby died. I mourned for him too but

your loss was so much deeper, only a mother can know. Now there is another boy. I could say that I wished he had never been born but what good would that do? I have undertaken to pay for Hajom's education. Miss Barr has kindly taken responsibility for him. Dear Margaret, my wife, I hope and pray we can put the past behind us and face the future together. I want to care for you and, in whatever way I can, to make up for the humiliation and hurt that I have caused you.

Your loving husband, Wallace

The letter is in his pocket when he goes to the railway station. Margaret phoned to tell him she was coming home. The line was bad, her voice distorted, but her instructions clear: he is not to come and meet her at the station, but Wallace cannot stay away. The thought that she might abandon him haunts him. He paces on the platform until the Belfast train comes to a belching standstill. Through the sooty clouds of smoke, Margaret emerges. To Wallace she cuts a forlorn figure. She looks bewildered. *I told you not to come ...'* but she doesn't object when he takes the suitcase from her and links her arm. The first time we were introduced, all those years ago, I was in awe of her independent spirit, he thinks. Now she seems fragile.

'Let's go to the Gresham Hotel for afternoon tea,' he says.

When they were first married, Wallace could not afford to bring his wife for a meal in the Gresham. Now everything is different. A brand-new motor car is parked outside the station. Without waiting for a reply, he ushers Margaret down the steps of the station and she comes with him, uncomplaining, into the ferocious noises of the street.

Once they are on the pavement she pushes him away. She steps back, her shoulders hunched. Like a tiger, he thinks, ready to spring. Under her narrow, felt hat, her eyes glitter.

'Margaret, please ...'

A growl escapes from her throat. 'How *could* you?'

Where to begin?

'With a servant, how could you? To stoop so low.'

She raises her gloved hand to strike him. Now it is his turn to step back, startled, the suitcase slipping from his hand. She swoops down and grabs it, brushing away his outstretched hand.

'My dearest.'

'You can keep your cream tea and your motor car.' Her voice crackles. 'I am going home on the tram.'

In the house in St Kevin's Park, an uneasy calm prevails. The girls are too busy chattering to be aware of the gulf that has opened up between Wallace at one end of the table, Margaret at the other.

'You missed it, Mummy, the parade,' Elizabeth says. 'It was enormously long.'

'It wasn't a parade, silly.' Her older sister counters. 'It was a *procession* with lots of ladies wearing white veils and singing hymns.'

Alexa nestles in close to her mother. 'I liked the man dressed up in the gold cloak and the fancy parasol the men carried for him. He looked like a wizard.'

Margaret turns, swivel-eyed, to Wallace. 'Do you mean to tell me that you brought the girls to a Roman Catholic procession?'

Wallace looks uncomfortable. 'Some folk from Seacon were coming down for the day and I thought I might meet up with them but the crowds were tremendous so I never did.'

Margaret is incredulous. 'From Seacon?'

'They came for the spectacle, I suppose. It was to celebrate the Centenary of Catholic Emancipation. A hundred years since 1829. You have to give it to the Roman

Catholics; they know how to put on a good show. There was papal bunting hanging from every lamp post.'

'And you brought our girls to see the *show*.'

A wintry silence. She tidies her knife and fork on her plate, dabs her mouth with a napkin. 'It seems to me, Wallace, that you have completely lost your wits.'

After the girls have gone upstairs to bed, and the maid comes in to clear the dishes, Wallace pushes back his chair and says, 'Margaret, we need to talk.'

In the drawing room a log fire is burning in the grate. At the sight of the faded, upholstered armchairs, the Indian teak bureau, the carved elephants on the mantelpiece, he thinks: you and I can resolve it here where we belong, in the home we have made together.

She is unyielding. *I don't want to hear your excuses ...*

He tries a different tack. 'The boy's name is Hajom.'

She refuses to listen. In an untypically theatrical gesture, she covers her ears. Then she weeps. The longer it goes on, the worse it gets: her face white and pinched, her head swaying, as she babbles through his expressions of regret.

When she stands up, he cannot look at her.

'You've betrayed everyone: me and the girls, the memory of our son. *My* son,' she says, rubbing the tears from her cheeks. 'Even God you've betrayed, Wallace McKay, when you exposed the children to that superstitious codswallop. You might as well have tied them up in papal bunting while you were at it.'

She brushes past him and slams the door behind her.

Wallace's frustration is tinged with admiration. The sight of her standing, broken and confused, on the railway platform, is like a dream. After so many years of marriage, he still doesn't have the measure of his wife's spirit. A sudden chill runs down his spine. Living so long in India has made him susceptible to the damp and cold of Dublin. He hurries down the steps to the kitchen to where the range has been banked for the night. Its residual warmth is inviting: comfort for his bones, a reminder of Seacon. What a battle he had to convince his mother to move out of the old farmhouse. Still, the new house is a success, particularly the modern kitchen, even if his mother complains that she's bamboozled by all the cupboards. *I canna find a thing I'm looking for ...*

A coal winks brightly in the ashes when Wallace opens the door of the range and throws in the letter. He watches as the edges of the pages curl up and burn. What a fool he was to write it and a bigger fool to expect Margaret to read it. It is a salve for his bad conscience, nothing more. The realisation sickens him. While the truth may be his, Margaret has justice on her side.

XX

'Where is Mr Carmody today?'

Wallace looks around at the cold, lean faces. An icy wind cuts across the fields. Shrugs and mutterings all around him. He has come to depend on the foreman. Sean Carmody keeps order in the allotments, yells at the slackers, curses like a sailor. The men like and respect him, so why isn't there a peep out of them now?

'I'll just have to go and find him myself.'

Wallace stumps off to the office to get the man's address. After his day is over, instead of taking the tram home he crosses the city until he reaches Denzille Street, a long narrow street that runs parallel to Merrion Square. Its once grand houses are now decaying tenements. The elegance of Merrion Square is a stone's throw away but a world apart. In the street the noise is deafening: the screams of children playing, the women shouting from the windows, the roll of cartwheels on the cobbles. He has no way of knowing which house he is looking for, but when he asks a young girl where Sean Carmody lives she points at a nearby entrance.

Third stairs up. Her face brightens as the coin he proffers disappears into her pocket.

Under a shattered fanlight, the hallway stretches into darkness. Wallace hesitates. This is unknown territory. He checks for his wallet, and finds it safe in an inner pocket. Reassured, he keeps going. His curiosity is whetted: he has seen many strange places in the world and now, in the heart of Dublin city, here is an opening to a foreign world. Working with the men on the allotments, he knows they come from the slums, but he knows nothing of the broken windows, the rotting walls, the foul stench of sewers.

Through an open door off the hallway there is a high-ceilinged room, a filthy curtain hanging over a mattress, clothes mounded on the floor, potato skins curling in a tin bucket, and, staring at him, a woman, hair dishevelled, a baby on her hip.

The staircase groans under his feet. For safety, he grasps the banister. It wobbles as he climbs. On the first landing, to his surprise, two men are standing with their backs to him. He stops, uncertain whether to go on or not, but the men are oblivious of his presence. Without speaking, they continue, almost dreamily, to gaze up the cavernous height of the stairwell.

'What is it?'

Silence answers him. The older man turns around. A not unfriendly gaze, an incurious examination of the stranger, before his attention drifts away. Wallace looks upwards and sees what they see: a long bundle dangling from a rope tied to a banister. On the next landing, another man is sawing through the rope.

'What is it?'

As the rope starts to fray, the bundle turns slowly, revealing itself to be a man in shirt sleeves, trousers and bare feet. His face is sunk onto his shoulder. Wallace rushes forward to join the two men just as the rope snaps and the body hurtles down through a rush of air into their outstretched arms. Under the sudden weight, he staggers against the rickety banister and prays that it will hold. He is conscious of the older man stumbling to his knees in a coughing fit. And of the younger one – just a boy – who manages to keep his balance and, wild-eyed with fear, is gripping the body to his scrawny chest as he collapses backwards down the stairs.

'Oh Jesus, Mary and Joseph.' The boy's screams stop only when Wallace comes down the stairs to him.

'Easy now,' he murmurs. 'Easy, easy now.'

Between them, they carry the body back up the stairs: the boy holding it under the arms, Wallace holding the legs. When they reach the landing, the older man is waiting for them. The boy closes his eyes and sways.

'Let me help you,' Wallace says, gently prising the boy's fingers open to let the body slide onto the floor. From the boy's throat comes a shuddering sound. The man who cut the rope comes down from the upper floor to join them. Four men and a body: the landing is crowded.

'He's dead as mutton,' the older man says.

'Poor soul, poor soul,' Wallace kneels down. He examines the blackened neck, the protruding tongue, the swollen cheeks. He looks for a pulse in the man's wrist but he knows it is hopeless. The man's eyes are wide open and staring. Gently, Wallace closes Sean Carmody's eyes, and lets his hand rest on the dead man's cheek. The transformation of man to corpse is a shock and yet Wallace feels disembodied: he is above the scene somehow, looking down. What is wrong with me he wonders? It is as if everything is happening at the other end of a telescope.

'Let us pray,' Wallace is embarrassed by the sound of his voice breaking the silence. The three men kneel down without a murmur. They pray together but their version of the Lord's Prayer is different to his, and their supplication ends in a jumble of words. Even in death we are divided, Wallace thinks, Protestant and Catholic. He stands up, brushes down his trousers. As he picks his hat up off the floor, he notices the dead man's naked feet.

He turns to the waiting men. 'Where are his boots?'

The older man's face is gaunt, a few thin wisps of hair on his head, a gummy grin. The other man stays in the shadows, indistinct and mute. The boy looks away.

'I have never seen Sean Carmody without his boots.'

The older man shrugs, takes a cigarette butt from behind his ear. 'Got a match, sir?'

'No, I have not,' Wallace says coldly.

The man gazes down at the cigarette butt in his hand. 'I would say now that some gurrier robbed them. There is nothing sacred around here.'

'Toe rags,' the boy pipes up, 'to be robbing a dead man.'

'But how is it possible?' Wallace asks. There is no reply.

Why must he always need to know the how and why of everything? The man is dead. Let him rest in peace. Wallace remembers that a Catholic priest goes hard in such circumstances. Sean Carmody was a good man and deserves a decent funeral.

'Has he a wife, children?'

'Four, so he has.'

'Maybe I should call on her.'

'Ah no, sir, no,' the older man says. 'We can manage from here on in.' Then slyly, 'But maybe, a bit of help for the widow?'

'Of course.' Wallace digs into his pocket. 'I don't want to intrude. Please give her this with my deepest condolences.'

The man pockets the money.

'She'd be in no state, sir, to have an Englishman calling.'

Wallace feels his face grow hot. He straightens up to his full height. How can anyone be so ignorant?

'Sorry, sir,' the older man mutters, 'ah, I'm sorry, sorry.'

Wallace lowers his voice. Looks around him. The others wait expectantly.

'I'll have you know,' he says, 'I am every bit an Irishman, as much as you are.'

The garden railings, the open gate, the rosebushes tied against the red brick wall, the glow of the hall light in the stained-glass panels of the front door. Wallace has never been more glad to arrive home. His only desire is to shut out the memory of the dead eyes of his foreman. To sit down by the fire and read a book. The new Eimar O'Duffy will do nicely. It will take him out of himself.

He finds Margaret at work in the scullery, wearing a long apron wrapped around her waist; her hair is swept into a hairnet. As she bends over an old porcelain sink, she is illuminated by a beam of light from the rusting skylight. It is a scene painted by a Dutch old master: the housewife in her element while he is the intruder. Unaware of his presence, Margaret continues to wash glass jars in preparation for making jam. In the garden, the loganberries and blackcurrants are ripening. The time will soon come when she'll dragoon the family into picking them before the birds plunder the fruit bushes. When she crouches down to get a cloth from a shelf below the sink, her rear swells inside her skirt. Ripe as fruit, he thinks, and as sweet.

'What are you doing?'

'What does it look like?'

He sighs. 'Let me help you.'

She turns and looks at him.

'Please.' Before she can object, he takes the cloth from her and starts to dry a jam jar.

'No, I've only washed them to get the dust off. The jars need to be sterilised.'

There is no animosity in her voice. After weeks of hostilities, he is grateful for the hint of a truce.

'I can do that.' Wallace says before she changes her mind.

In the kitchen a large saucepan of water is bubbling on the stove. He stacks jam jars on a tray and then carries the laden tray into the kitchen. At first, they work in silence: Margaret washes the jam jars at the sink, Wallace carries them into the kitchen and plunges them, one by one, into the boiling water. Fishing them out of the saucepan is more difficult, he discovers, entailing some expletives on his part. At one point, he accidentally puts his hand in the boiling water and dances around the kitchen, squawking with pain.

Hearing the commotion, Margaret rushes in from the scullery, crying, 'Heavens, are you codding me or what?'

He hangs his head. 'It's nothing, nothing at all.'

'Come here to the sink.' She takes his hand and puts it under the running tap. For a time, they stand, side by side, their hands entwined. It is the first time they have touched in months. The heat of his hand is supplanted by the iciness of the water. He is inured to pain. The soothing gush from the tap and the sound of her laughter are balm to his soul.

'Margaret,' he says, 'I've had a terrible day.'

They sit down together at the kitchen table. She dabs disinfectant on his burnt hand and dresses it with gauze, while he recounts his visit to Denzille Street. He tells her every detail: he has already decided that he will never again lie to his wife, about anything.

'Oh, Wallace,' she says when he has finished, 'it must have been terrifying.'

'Not terrifying, no,' he says. 'I was a bit shaken, that is true but I was completely calm. I don't know why. I wasn't alone – there were two local men there and the boy. Poor chap, he was rather cut up but I didn't feel anything much. Strange, in a way, how detached I felt.'

'Do you know what my sister, Jane, calls the two of us?'

He looks puzzled.

'Ice and fire. I don't have to tell you which one is the ice.'

He gives a wry smile. His sister-in-law is right. He is done with emotions: they only get a man into trouble.

'I closed poor Sean Carmody's eyes. I won't forget that look of his.'

'I wonder,' she murmurs, 'what drove him to kill himself.'

But Wallace isn't listening. 'Come to think of it, the only time that I felt anything at all was when the men took me for an Englishman.'

She stops packing away the roll of gauze and bottle of disinfectant into a drawer.

'An Englishman? Why on earth?'

He shrugs, flattens his bandaged hand on the table. 'Explains the difference between them and me, I suppose. An Ulsterman, you know. They don't know any better.'

'And you are a Unitarian.'

He remembers the prayer on the dim landing. 'Yes.'

A troubled look in her face, as if she has something to say and is half-afraid to say it. She pulls the hairnet off her head and plays with it between her fingers.

'What is it?'

'Oh, it's nothing.'

'Now, Margaret, it is not nothing. You can tell me.'

Her reply is barely audible. 'It's just that I wonder sometimes, about this country.'

Wallace waits.

'Whether you and I belong here at all,' she says in a rush.

This is something he never expected to hear: Margaret has always been unstinting in her support for the new State. Her allegiance has got her into a few quarrels over the years. By contrast, he is phlegmatic by nature: he has learnt not to argue with the loyal daughter of Erin he is married to, or with anyone else for that matter. If he is ice, as his sister-in-law maintains, then Margaret is fire. It has been so from the beginning.

'I have never heard you say anything like that before.'

Her face is impassive. Her fingers pick at the hairnet.

'Are you unhappy here, my dearest?'

What a stupid question, he thinks. Of course she is, and it is his fault.

'It's very difficult sometimes. At the bridge game last night we were talking. It was just a silly conversation, but you wouldn't believe how disagreeable those people can be. West Britons, every single one. I wouldn't mind: I was being perfectly reasonable. All I said was that if they didn't like living in the Free State they could emigrate. It sent them into a right tizzy.' She looks gloomy. 'After that, the evening went from bad to worse.'

She senses his amusement, withdraws her hand and sits up straight. 'I told them I wouldn't play cards with them ever again.'

'But you love bridge!'

'I have my principles.'

In Dublin, their circle of friends is small, built around the church on St Stephen's Green. In winter there are evenings of entertainment, in summer, picnics in county Wicklow and walks in the hills. Wallace is away so much for work, Margaret depends on the members of the congregation for company. No wonder she is upset. He wishes he could find something to say to comfort her.

'Margaret ...'

She stands up, brushes down her apron.

'My mind is made up,' she says. 'Now I have to finish the jam jars.'

Soon there are rows of jam jars gleaming on a shelf in the larder. Margaret comes into the kitchen carrying a full kettle. With her elbow, she nudges Wallace away from the range, where he is warming himself. 'Out of my way.'

He obliges, smiling.

'At last,' with a satisfied sigh, she puts the kettle on a hot plate, 'we'll have a nice cup of cha.'

When the girls come in from school, they find their parents sitting in the kitchen. It is not often they see Wallace in his shirt-sleeves, Margaret is wearing her apron. Their air of settled informality is tantalising.

'It's the maid's afternoon off,' Margaret explains. 'We are having tea in the kitchen so you can all pitch in.'

He sits and smokes his pipe while the girls set the table and Margaret cuts slabs of a floury loaf. She brings to the table the platter piled up with slices of bread, lifts the big tin teapot and pours tea into the enamel mugs before she sits down at the head of the table.

'There's the last of the year's jam, Marmite and fish paste,' she says, 'so you can take your pick.'

Wallace looks around the kitchen: everything is in its place, the crockery on the dresser, the kettle on the range, the jam jars in the larder, the spread board. Aye, he thinks, she will never leave me. She belongs here. The queen bee is in her hive.

Maggie takes delicate bites when she eats, sips from her mug and dabs her mouth with her napkin, while the two younger girls sprawl, their elbows on the table and chatter like monkeys.

'Manners!' their mother says, but the girls are too busy talking to pay any attention. Margaret throws up her hands in mock despair. Wallace catches her eye. Her faint smile gives him a moment's hope. But, before he can say anything, she turns away, her face closed up, shutter-like.

XXI

1938

Everything is different now. Margaret isn't nostalgic for the old days under the yoke of the British empire. Being Irish is a matter of pride but she is no longer sure what being Irish means. There is a shift taking place. At times it is imperceptible and, at other times, manifest. The transformation of Dublin for the Eucharistic Congress is a cause of great unease. The multitude of people in the streets, the garlanded statues of Mary, the flags and banners, the ceremonial arches, there is no escape from the religious fervour, the cloying atmosphere of piety. Why must they clog up the streets, Margaret wondered. Why can't they pray inside their churches in the way that decent people do?

During her time in Calcutta she had observed similar outbursts of ardour: the tawdry decoration of Hindu temples; the masses of chanting followers, the sickly sweet flowers. Paganism, Popery. There is no difference that she can see. A people in thrall to superstition. Such displays were commonplace in India but she never expected to see them in her beloved Ireland.

When she was a teacher, the Jewish children taught her a saying: 'Life is a narrow bridge between two eternities, you must have courage.' The saying has served her well. Through all the dangers she faced in India: the snakes and wild animals, the terrible food, sickness, the mosquitoes, she was without fear. That was her protection. Now she feels her courage seeping away as the ground sinks beneath her. Each year on her dead son's birthday she is flayed by the thoughts of what might have been. Had he lived he would be a young man now: a fitting coda, while the other one, the Indian one, is a laceration that refuses to heal.

Margaret feels threatened on all sides. Ireland is becoming an alien country. The influence of Rome is spreading like weeds colonising a herbaceous border. She attends Sunday service in the hope of solace and pays close attention to the minister's sermon. This week the title of his sermon is 'Living in a Changing World.'

'Unitarians have battled for religious liberty all down the centuries and the liberty they have sought for themselves they have claimed for others,' the minister says. 'They were amongst the foremost supporters of Catholic emancipation.'

After the service is over, the congregation gathers to drink tea together downstairs. Margaret makes her way through the crowd. She is determined to put the minister right.

'Your sermon ...'

He turns to her, smiling.

'It seems to me when it comes to change,' she comes close to him, 'these days, we Irish have succeeded in trading the rule of one empire for another one.'

His face furrows in dismay.

'I mean the Church of Rome. If the Kingdom of Heaven is inside each one of us, then surely there is no need of bishops parading the streets and government ministers queuing up to kiss their rings.'

Answer that, Reverend. Come to think of it, with his high-domed head and fleshy cheeks, he could be mistaken for a bishop himself. The minister munches on a biscuit and looks thoughtful.

'My dear lady,' he says, 'there are many people who think they have a monopoly on truth.'

His gnomic reply confounds her long enough for him to vanish into the crowd. She looks around her: there is no one else who will listen.

In Shillong, she had read in *The Freeman's Journal* about Protestants being murdered and their houses burned to the ground. She hadn't understood what it meant. From a distance halfway across the world she dismissed those stories. How flippant she was in those days! Her vision of a nation freed from the shackles of empire trumped everything. The wellspring of a new Ireland, she was sure, would be hope and liberty.

And now.

'It seems to me,' she says to Wallace on one of his trips home, 'that far from being governed by hope and liberty, the nation is now ruled by a pope and *Ne Temere*. I must say that I never expected that Protestants would be squeezed like the pips from a lemon.'

For once, Wallace does not disagree. He folds up his newspaper and looks at her. 'Does it bother you?'

She bridles. 'I've every right to be bothered.'

'Yes, but you are free to believe whatever you like. No one wants to change your mind.'

'I'd like to see them try.'

He is losing interest.

'Can't you see,' she wants to say, 'we are caught in a net of laws and a constitution designed to circumscribe our very existence?'

'We are no petty people,' Wallace says, 'to quote Mr Yeats.'

That is so trite, she thinks, and no help at all. She opens up her sewing basket, takes out a needle and is busy threading it.

Her response is caustic. 'Oh yes, Wallace, I've no doubt that Mr de Valera will see us in that light.'

She plunges her needle into a border of yellow-hearted daisies. The air in the drawing room is dusty and stale. Rain beats against the window. A petal falls from a vase of flowers on the piano. The afternoon somnolence reminds her of Elderslie during the monsoon season. And if we are fooling ourselves about the future, she thinks what then?

'Remind me again, why did we decide to come home?'

'Because of the girls' education,' her husband answers, 'and because it is home.'

But it doesn't feel like home anymore, she wants to say.

Once she starts looking for signs, they are everywhere. Her favourite magazine, *The Picture Post* stops being delivered from England long ago. When she goes into Hodges Figgis Bookshop she is informed that the book she asked for is no longer available.

'What do you mean, not available? I'm looking for a book by George Bernard Shaw.'

The old man at the counter shakes his head. He looks tired, as if he's had this conversation too many times with his customers.

'He's our foremost Irish writer. He won the Nobel Prize for Literature.'

He is apologetic but firm. 'The Board of Censors ...'

Slapping her hand on the counter, she glares at him, 'I would also like to buy the new Aldous Huxley book.'

It is not true: she has no intention of buying the Aldous Huxley book. She's heard that it is coarse and sensational, not the kind of book she would ever read, but that is not the point. If she *did* want to read the Huxley book she would do so without hesitation. Her conscience would be her guide and not some stupid law.

'Didn't Jesus teach that laws were made for Man,' she says, 'and not the other way around?

The bookshop assistant takes off his spectacles and rubs his eyes with his knuckles. 'Ah, now, Mrs McKay.'

She is merciless. 'The title of the book I'm looking for is *Brave New World.*'

When Margaret gets home, her middle daughter is at the receiving end of her ire. Elizabeth is beautiful, sallow-skinned, with dreamy eyes and a languid air. There are times when her mother wants to give her a good shake.

'One of these days, Elizabeth, you're to stop your gadding about and settle down. Otherwise you'll end up an old maid.'

'Gosh!' Her daughter is wide-eyed. 'Do you think I'm old?'

'Well, you're not getting any younger.'

'But, Mummy, you said you were thirty-one when you married Daddy. I'm only twenty-six.'

'That's different,' her mother says. 'You need to get yourself a husband. A man who will look after you.'

'But Mummy, you said we should be able to look after ourselves.'

Did she say that? Margaret cannot remember. If she did, it was long before the fault lines appeared on the political landscape. Before she lost her innocence about life in the Free State. Now she understands what must be done. From now on, her daughters need to be safely ensconced with their own kind.

'Don't be silly, Elizabeth.' She purses her lips. 'You will find that life is hard enough without making trouble for yourself. A nice, steady man with prospects is exactly what you need. Those Trinity College types you run around with, any one of those young men will suit.'

Elizabeth murmurs, 'Don't you think I should have a say in the matter?'

Once again, Wallace McKay leaves India behind: the regimented system of the tea garden where everyone knows their place; where he works all hours of the day and where he writes the book that he knows now will never be completed.

He shrugs off the heat and dust and travels by ship halfway across the world so that he can spend peace in his own home in Dublin, only to find when he opens his front door, that he is pitched, willy nilly, into a cauldron churning with emotions.

Margaret is waiting for him, swollen-faced and furious.

'I don't care how you do it, Wallace. You must get Elizabeth to see sense.'

Elizabeth, his second daughter, who is hiding in her bedroom, doodling in her sketch pad and dreaming of love.

He is calm. 'I will speak to her.'

And so, father and daughter go into his study. Firmly, he shuts the door in his wife's face. 'Leave the matter to me, Margaret, it is better this way.'

In his study, he casts a wistful eye on the letters on his desk waiting to be opened, then he concentrates on the task in hand.

'Elizabeth,' he says, 'your mother is very upset.'

'Well, I don't see why she is. Mummy told me to find a husband.'

Her sulkiness irritates him.

'You must have known that this marriage will not do,' he says sharply.

'I even found someone from Trinity College like she wanted.'

'You know your mother meant you were to find one of your own kind.'

Patiently Wallace starts to explain about the long shadow cast by the *Ne Temere* decree but Elizabeth interrupts him. 'I don't care about any of that, Daddy.'

He is momentarily at a loss.

'I'm disappointed to hear you say that.'

She shrugs.

'You should care, Elizabeth. This is important.'

Nothing can reach her: she is implacable. His daughter, Wallace realises, is a woman made of steel, just like her mother.

'It is really very simple, Daddy. Tim O'Driscoll has asked me to marry him and I have said yes.'

The two of them sit in silence until the sound of the dinner gong releases them. When they come out into the hall, Margaret is waiting.

'Believe me,' he tells her. 'I did try.'

'Clearly, not hard enough,' she says.

To escape the atmosphere in the house, the arguments and threats, the banging doors, Wallace drives to Seacon to visit his mother. The old woman has become an invalid, ruling the household from her bed. Anna leads him to her mother's bedroom. Mam has the sheets destroyed, she tells him, the exercises she is doing, to keep her legs from seizing up.

When he enters, his mother struggles up in the bed to greet him. Her face has collapsed into old age, her eyes sunken under the weight of their lids. He talks and she is content to listen, until he finds the courage to tell her his news.

Her reaction is ferocious. 'That woman has lost the run of herself.'

'Now, Mam, please!'

'She is your wife, you must get her to see reason. To disown her own child, it's outrageous. What on earth are you thinking, Wallace?'

'Mam, my head is cracked from thinking.'

Silence.

When she speaks, her voice is full of repressed anger. 'If Elizabeth wants to marry a papist, then so be it. Any religion is better than none, surely. She is a grown woman. Family, children, grandchildren. Ach, for the good Lord's sake, that is all that matters. Blood is thicker than water. You know that, haven't I said it often enough?'

He smiles sadly. 'Aye, you have.'

'Well, that daft targe you married should know it too.'

'It's not so easy.'

Exasperated, his mother falls back on the pillows. She glares up at him.

'I should have stopped you from marrying *her* when I had the chance.'

XXII

When the church door opens, Margaret doesn't recognise the elderly minister standing before her. With his tousled hair he resembles a startled squirrel, nervous and whiskered.

He is cheerful. 'The boss is away, so I'll have to do, I'm afraid, until he returns from his holiday. Come in, come in.'

He pulls the door to, then blows on his cupped hands and rubs them. 'The heating's broken down again. We'll talk downstairs.'

They descend the stone staircase and into the schoolroom. Smells of damp and polish catapult her into a time when there was only herself there, and the schoolchildren in her care, their faces upturned to the light coming through the big windows and singing, *Oft in the stilly night* while, behind her hand, she smiled at the sound of their thick Lithuanian vowels.

'Shall we sit down?' he says.

She has already forgotten his name. Thompson? Grigson?

She sits down at the teacher's desk and runs her finger along the edge, bringing up dust on the pad of her forefinger. Some things don't change. She gazes down at the rows of forms where the children used to sit. We grow up, grow old and die. She is no different, so why does she care so much? She could be like some others, who are quiescent, hunkering down while the world grows colder around them.

'Now tell me what's on your mind.'

She speaks without emotion. Tells him everything. He must understand that she is making a reasonable case. The sound of her voice is louder than she expects, bouncing off the walls of the schoolroom. Just like it did, she remembers, in the old days.

'Please believe me,' she is earnest in her plea, 'this matter has nothing to do with religion. Roman Catholics can worship the nearest railway station for all I care. It is the laws of their hierarchy. They are solely designed to increase their power. I never tell them what to do, so why do they think they must tell me what I can do?'

'I see.'

'And now, my daughter wants to marry one of them. I will not permit it. To be married in a Catholic church is one thing but to be forced to hand the children she will have into the clutches of Rome. It is unconscionable.'

Again, he says that he sees.

Hearing her thoughts spoken aloud invests them with authority and, conversely, in the pit of her stomach with a new anxiety. What if she fails?

'I want you to put a stop to it.'

He looks thoughtful and spreads his fingers on the table. 'My dear.'

'Please, you must,' she says. 'Please ...'

To her horror, she can sense that he is backing away. Not physically – not a muscle moves – but in his mind.

'Your daughter is a grown woman,' he murmurs. 'Her conscience must be her guide. That is a precept of our church, remember? Our sons and daughters choose their own paths and will learn from their mistakes. We must not threaten or force them to do otherwise.'

He is dewy-eyed with sympathy, but it is obvious: the minister has no intention of getting enmeshed in a family quarrel.

Her voice cracks. 'And must we not fight superstition?'

She squints down at the books heaped on the desk. Sewell's English poetry, a mathematics primer. Old textbooks that are familiar to her.

She must not cry. No matter what.

With a sigh, the minister struggles to stand up. 'Come with me, Mrs McKay.'

His tone is solicitous. His arthritic fingers grip her arm as she helps him up. Without speaking, she follows him upstairs and waits while he unlocks the door, then stands aside to let her enter.

How strange, she thinks, to see the church empty of people, the rows of pews expectant. Looming above the pulpit, is the newly-installed stained glass window, enormous and glowing, as sunlight pours through its coloured panes. She has grown to love this window. It often distracts her when she attends the Sunday service. Each panel in the window represents a theme: Discovery. Truth. Love. Work. Each one is important enough to satisfy her inquisitive mind. And in the centre, the pinnacle of thought: Inspiration.

Once they are settled in the front pew, the minister turns to her. 'My dear, have no doubt about it, you will find the strength to endure this trial.'

Is he about to give her a sermon? Yes.

'In this church,' he continues, 'is a legacy of freedom of thought, of progressive thought, of aspiration, praise and prayer. It is a great tradition, a free gift from a splendid past. It's for you, Mrs McKay, for us all. The age old heart hunger of mankind for communion with the Eternal and the vision of things spiritual, abides, implanted in the soul of humanity. In time, the present state of your confusion will merge into a deeper faith, a truer outlook, a wider charity.'

No.

He whispers, 'Let us pray now.'

He steeples his fingers and bends his head. Margaret sits upright, her eyes travelling across the stained glass window. Slowly, she absorbs each image, before moving on to the next one.

Discovery is a scientist working at his experiment.

Love is a mother, a baby on her breast, two children at her feet.

Work is a blacksmith in his forge.

And, at last, the one Margaret seeks out: a woman clad in armour and ready to fight, standing on a rocky path. Her heel placed on a serpent. Above her head, she raises a torch that streams fire out across the sky.

The flame of Truth.

The minister is wrong: Margaret's current state is not confusion. She is absolutely clear-headed. She will not give way. This is how one must live: true to one's conscience. The way the martyrs lived. She won't be crushed by memories of the past. Once upon a time she believed that Ireland would be reborn, pure and free. She knows now that that is a fairy story, a dream. Sickness has taken root in the country and Margaret recognises the pain that such sickness brings. She knows very well that it is the worst pain of all: to have a new life snuffed out before her eyes.

I have known betrayal, she vows, but I will not be a traitor.

She wants to assure the minister of this but when she looks around she finds there is nobody there. The church is empty. She hears a muffled shout from below: 'Just a mo'. Forgot to turn off the lights. Sorry!'

As daylight fades, the stained glass window darkens and an icy air coils around her. She feels an ache of loneliness: a sudden kick of anguish under her breast. For a moment, as if new life is growing inside her, she feels a tiny foot pressing against the wall of her womb.

'Oh Elizabeth,' Margaret mourns. 'My sweet, darling child.'

She covers her face with her hands and weeps.

The minister returns to find her standing in the doorway.

'My dear Mrs McKay.' He raises his hands helplessly.

She turns her tear-stained face towards him.

'Reverend Thompson, or whatever your name is, I will not forget. When I came to my pastor looking for help, you refused me.'

In the street a tram passes by, packed with people. The thunder of automobiles and carts and, above the noise, the dusty air is edged with birdsong. She is filled with an inexplicable urge to sing. A concluding hymn, if she can think of one. She bangs the tip of her umbrella on the pavement. A perfect cue. Ah yes, here is one she knows.

Hope on, hope on, the golden days
Are not as yet a-dawning;

Lord, what's the next line, something about mists, Ah yes.

The mists of night precede the light,
And usher in the morning.

She sings lustily as she walks along, beating out the rhythm with her umbrella and ignoring the amused glances of the passersby, the child pulling on his mother's sleeve and pointing to the dotty lady making a show of herself. Margaret doesn't care about any of them. She is determined to keep singing, even if she can't remember the words. She is determined, too, never to set her foot inside the Unitarian church on St Stephen's Green again.

A sports car is parked outside the house in St Kevin's Park. Trudging up from the corner of the road, Margaret sees two young men leaning against the car, in camel hair coats and tweed caps, cigarette smoke curling up from their fingers. Any minute now, her long-legged daughters will spill out of the house. And here they come, just as she expected: Maggie and Alexa. She is still too far away to do anything except to observe them clambering into the sports car, and the young men jumping in after them. Car doors slam, the ignition roars, smoke pours out of the exhaust pipe. They too are leaving me, Margaret thinks, and one day it will be for good. She is startled by a blare of the car horn, the waving hands and screams of excitement as they roar past her.

When she opens the front door Margaret senses the absence. There is nobody else in the silent house. The girls have gone, Wallace is away, and the maid is out. Even the cat is away, hunting in the hedges for a mouse or bird to torment before leaving it for dead on the kitchen step. An innocent casualty.

Postscript

My father, Timothy O'Driscoll, was a student at Trinity College Dublin when he met and fell in love with my mother, Elizabeth, the middle daughter of Wallace and Margaret McKay. Although he was a devout Catholic, he had a mind of his own. The Catholic bishops had decreed that it was a mortal sin at that time for a Catholic parent to send their child to study in Trinity College. My father considered himself safe from the threat of hellfire because, since he was a full-time civil servant, he was putting himself through college as a night student. He, and not his parents, was paying his fees, so he reckoned that the ban did not apply to him.

Getting married, he discovered, was a more daunting challenge. When it came to the wedding, Timothy was governed by the conditions set out in the papal *Ne Temere* decree. This required that the couple be married by a priest in a Catholic church. To his dismay, church after church in Dublin refused his request. Eventually, a priest in the Whitehall parish took pity on him and agreed to officiate at the wedding.

Because it was 'a mixed marriage' (between a Catholic and a Protestant) the wedding was held in a side chapel, with a few friends and relatives in attendance. Before the ceremony began, the priest was taken aback to discover that the bride was not baptised. When he learnt that the witness, Alexa, Elizabeth's sister and maid of honour, was not baptised either, he refused to proceed with the wedding.

The priest's announcement caused consternation among the little gathering. For a while it looked like the marriage ceremony would be aborted. Then one of the guests came to the rescue of the young couple: a Presentation brother in Cork, who had taught my father in secondary school and had taken a particular interest in his student's progress. In the hiatus, he tugged on the bridegroom's sleeve.

'Give him five pounds,' he whispered. 'That should take care of it.'

More in hope than expectation, my father complied. The money changed hands. The ceremony went ahead and my parents left the church in Whitehall, a lawfully-wedded couple. I have a photograph that was taken on the day. The bride is dressed in a plaid wartime suit and wears her hat at an elegant angle. The groom has opened the door of a taxi for her. Her foot is on the running board. Before getting into the taxi, the newly-married couple smile into the camera lens. Their joy is tinged, I imagine, with a feeling of relief.

Timothy O'Driscoll and Elizabeth McKay went on to have a family of three daughters. They were happily married for over fifty years.

Theirs, you might say, was a marriage made in heaven.

When she married my father, my mother sloughed off her past. Circumstances demanded that she recreate herself and start a new life. My mother lived in the moment. She wasn't interested in reminiscing. My parents did not discuss religion: at least, they never did so in front of their daughters. As was required, my sisters and I were raised in the Catholic faith, but it didn't stick. By the time we were adults, each one of us had drifted away from organised religion of any kind. The rift between my mother and her parents was never healed, although, for the rest of her life, Elizabeth kept up contact with her two sisters.

Eventually my grandparents, Wallace and Margaret McKay, left Dublin for good and settled in London. In 1945 he was appointed to the board of directors of the Assam Tea company. On retirement my grandparents went to live in Hastings in the south of England. They both died in 1967. Margaret spent her last days in Gloucester hospital. When she was dying, according to her eldest daughter (my Aunt Margaret) my grandmother cried out, 'When is Daddy coming back? He's gone up the hills to that woman, and he's been gone a long time.'

That woman was Margaret Barr, the Unitarian minister who refused to be called a missionary. She was the only Westerner to have care of Wallace's son. The existence of the boy was a well-kept secret. My mother, Elizabeth, was an old woman when she first learnt of her half-brother's existence. We made attempts to find him, but without success. The Khasi lineage is matrilineal which makes tracing impossible. Aunt Margaret made a few fruitless efforts. My youngest son, Sam, visited Shillong but was unable to find any record of his great-uncle.

In 2016 I went to stay in that hilly, straggling city in northern India. Shillong's streets are choked with traffic now, but it is surrounded, even today, by magnificent forests. I visited each of the two Unitarian churches that continue to flourish there. In the courtyard of one church stands a bust of Kissor Singh and, in a meeting room, there is a framed photograph of Margaret Barr. Among the

Meghalayan hills, the school she founded still bears her name.

Kong Barr, I learnt, is remembered there with great affection.

I like to think that my grandparents found contentment in their old age. On one occasion, my aunt Margaret (Maggie) visited them in their flat in London, and afterwards she wrote to my mother about her visit. Reading her letter, I can visualise the elderly couple in their small kitchen. Standing at the gas cooker, Wallace is stirring, with a wooden spoon, the contents of a large saucepan. He is making marmalade and the kitchen is rich with the smell of oranges. There are glass jam jars on the worktop waiting to be filled. His wife is sitting at the pull-out table. By that time, she has made a hobby of trading in stocks and shares. The *Financial Times* is open on the table and she is reading aloud from the daily stock market results.

In recent times the Unitarian church in Dublin has become a place of significance for me. My mother's funeral service was held in that church, as was my sister Sara's, and my grandson Danny's naming ceremony. I have grown to admire the pared-back nature of Unitarianism and the way that the church is an open house for the disenchanted. Sometimes I am asked what do Unitarians believe and, in my mind I hear the answer that I put into my grandmother's mouth:

> We do not subscribe to any creed. We depend on ourselves, on our intelligence, as well as on the guidance of reason and conscience to teach us how to live.

I cherish this way of thinking. It is a legacy that has been handed down to me by generations in my mother's family. Sadly, I never knew any of them, but, in writing this book, I have discovered a way of imagining two of them: my grandparents, John Wallace and Margaret McKay.

ABOUT THE AUTHOR

Born in Canada in 1947, Liz McManus was brought up in Dublin. She worked as an architect in Derry, Galway, Dublin and Wicklow, and was a newspaper columnist from 1985–1993. Her first novel, *Acts of Subversion* (Poolbeg Press, 1992), was shortlisted for the Aer Lingus/*Irish Times* Award for New Writing. Her second novel, *A Shadow in the Yard*, was published by Ward River Press in 2015.

Awards include a Hennessy New Irish Writing Award, Listowel Short Story Award and Irish PEN Award. She was conferred with an M.Phil in Creative Writing (Trinity College) in 2012, and is currently working on a Ph.D at the University of Limerick.

A parliamentarian for 19 years, she was Minister for Housing and Urban Renewal (1994–97) and Chairperson of the Taskforce on the Needs of Travellers. She has been a campaigner for women's rights and a Chairperson of the Board of the Irish Writers Centre.

nould thank that I am bound
grateful to those who read the
ne time to comment on it: John
unne, Jonathan Williams, Lia Mills,
eila and Fergus Whelan, and Andy
inkerton and Bill Macafee of Ballymoney.
ylward for sharing his expertise on tea
e Reverend Bridget Spain and Rory Delany of
en's Green Unitarian church for giving me time
pace. To the WEB group for being my treasured
panions along the way. To the Tyrone Guthrie Centre
County Monaghan for providing sanctuary when I
needed it, the Royal Irish Academy, to Brian Donnelly of
the National Archives of Ireland, and the National Library
of Ireland. To J.J. Dwyer and the kind people I met or
talked to in the Adabari tea estate in Assam and in
Shillong in Meghalaya, including Danny Parlat, Battinore
Rani, Derrick Pariat, Brian Daly, Sharon Menzies and her
family. In my own family I want to thank Wallace Russell,
his late sister Dorothy, and his wife, Rosemary Stephenson
for their help, my niece Kate Horgan for the photographs,
my sister Mary and my late sister Sara, who cared for our
late Aunt Margaret's papers so assiduously. To my
children Luke, Ronan, Sam and Emily and, in particular, to
my partner Sean who supported me through all the highs
and lows. And to Alan Hayes of Arlen House who has
kept the faith.